DON'T

TAKE IT PERSONALLY

by

BARBARA BAYLEY

For Cynthia

For Harold and Anne —
Enjoy !
Barb
4/13/19

1

From the poem "Richard Cory "

   by Edwin Arlington Robinson

Whenever Richard Cory went down town,

We people on the pavement looked at him:

He was a gentleman from sole to crown,

Clean favored, and imperially slim.

And he was always quietly arrayed,

And he was always human when he talked;

But still he fluttered pulses when he said,

"Good morning," and he glittered when he walked.

And he was rich—yes, richer than a king—

And admirably schooled in every grace;

In fine, we thought that he was everything

To make us wish that we were in his place . .

The Hills Outside My Window   Mayetta Jane McDowell   1984

The hills are like a patchwork quilt

In early days of fall

With red and gold and green and brown

That meet to form a scrawl

Of loveliness unequall-ed

That holds me in its thrall.

Oh cover me, thou beauteous quilt!

Beneath thee I would lie.

Come, cover me with rapture

One last time, before you die.

.

(First Prize Winner, Poetry Contest, 1984   Jerome High School, West Virginia)

3

One.

Maya (McDowell) Porter, 1:34 am, Friday, May 17, 2019   Banana Bay, Florida

Plunging, lunging, swooping, stooping, diving,

Pitching headlong, at once fighting against and being one with gravity,

The featherless falcon decides, rejoices   YES. YES! Can you not see? I was born for this!

Ag-h-h! I lurch into wakefulness, gasping for air as though I have been underwater holding my breath, pulling my twisted nightgown from around my throat. The black nightgown, the one I had thought so appealing, the one I bought to wear for Franklin when he returned from South Carolina after buying his boat and piloting it by himself back alone, assuring me he would hug the coastline. This nightgown that he never got to admire on my body before watching me ease it off for him with my eager hands.

I reach in the dark, searching the night table beside me for my cellphone and glasses. I check the time. Ugh--I've only been asleep an hour. Vodka is not that good as a sedative; I fall asleep and this always happens. And yet I have stayed devoted to my nightly solo drink for almost a year now.

Well. Whatever bad dream this was, it is now gone, as fleeting as a wisp of cloud. I think I was creating a poem, although now I can't remember the poem or its content. I really need to keep paper and pen beside our bed, even though the part of my brain that creates poems dried up when Franklin left.

I wait until my heart calms down, go into the bathroom, void (vodka seems to stimulate my kidneys), and then get a drink of water. I don't flip on the light—I don't want to have to look at my half-century-old face. The upkeep of the body has begun in earnest, starting at my head, which I'm sure would explode into gray hairs if I didn't keep having them "refreshed", as my hairdresser Julian explains it.

I throw my damp nightgown (I'm too old for menopause at fifty-two, I insist) into the basket on the floor of the closet, still crowded with Franklin's expensive suits and monogrammed shirts. I do this from smell and touch, not sight, not caring right now if the nightgown hits its target, and I feel for a fresh gown in my dresser drawer—the nightgown drawer at chest height, which is why I can do all this in the dark.

I plump my pillow and lie down on my side of the bed. No need to feel for Franklin—he has been gone for—oh!—as of 12:01 am, a half hour ago, exactly a year!—an anniversary of the most grotesque kind—he just *disappeared* out of our lives, with people trying to tell me that he went down when his boat that he was intending to name for his daughter Frances (*why not for me?*, a tiny piece of my brain asks*)*, caught fire and sank, a crowd of gawkers on the beach with binoculars even murmuring the dreaded word "shark" as the Coast Guard search plane circled the area and a Coast Guard boat mowed back and forth in the Atlantic searching for debris, with me on the shore putting my hands dramatically to my ears to let the curious know that I would not tolerate such scary thoughts.

Such poor photos they took of me! I was embarrassed that I should have such a self-centered thought at such a distressing time. I couldn't decide whether to keep them for Franklin to see when he returned, or to banish them from the house. I guess Frances didn't keep them for her father, she was so sure he was gone. I never came to a conclusion about saving the newspaper articles, which lauded Franklin's many contributions to the Banana Bay community, with various early spellings of my name: "Meya", "Maia", and one time in the Week End Shop Here News even "Mahler".

How Franklin would have laughed!

I never got to pretend to admire his boat, never saw even a photo of it. I would have been scared to go out in it with him, since I never learned to swim and only stay in the shallow end of our pool while grandson Frankie yells, splashing water on me and diving like a seal.

Maybe that's why he wasn't going to name it after me.

If Franklin were here I would now be snuggling against him and he would be whispering, hardly roused into awareness, "Bad dream, Maya?" and I would be saying in relief, "Yes, yes—I'm so glad you're here," and he would give me a hug with those strong arms of his, those Harvard champion swimmer's arms even at his age of fifty-seven (fifty-eight now, a birthday this past year gone with our not knowing whether to celebrate it or not), already back into sleep.

There are two reasons why I don't believe he drowned: he knows how to swim. I'm the only one who holds to this theory, though. I don't talk like this to Frances—she worships her father and can't bear the idea of my holding out hope. So—now it's been a year. No wonder the bad dream. And Franklin had me swear a few years ago that I would tell no one, not even our daughter, that he was working on a very hush-hush job for the government. Such top priority that there's no way the government would let him die, as far as I know.

There's another reason not to turn on the light: I don't want to have to study the battleship-gray walls.

Franklin loves gray. He let me do what I wanted (I'd never lived in a house this size. What decisions could I make that weren't better than Franklin's?) with the rest of the house, but he insisted on this color for our bedroom. He chose such an obvious way of letting me know he was in charge. Anyway, I've kept it this shade. He needs to see that some things are the same when he returns from—

I don't know where. I don't know when. I just know down deep in my West Virginia bones that he's still alive and coming home to me and Frances and Frankie.

Frankie—oh, now a shard of my dream comes back to me! In it I was a peregrine falcon, like the one my grandson and I had met while I was recently helping him do some third-grade research about raptors. At the bird sanctuary just north of Banana Bay we had seen birds in various states of recovery from illness or injury. Frankie got excited about the owls and their innocent comical faces; but I had been drawn to the large peregrine falcon, close to two feet tall, on the leathered wrist of one of the female attendants. Its feathers were greyish on the back, white on the chest. The bird's legs were muscular, the toes that grasped the perch powerful, made for gripping its victim.

Miss Betsy (her nametag said) took the hood from the bird's head (it was a female, which is larger than the male, Miss Betsy told us). The peregrine stared at me unblinking as though daring me to talk back to her, as though she were the ruler and I her slave, with those huge oversized eyes.

She beat her wings as the attendant soothed her. "See the beautiful dark feathers around her eyes? That reduces glare, so she can see to hunt better."

"Like a football player does!" Frankie tried to pet the bird, which pulled back, yanking on the cord attached to the perch and the bird's leg.

"Careful," Miss Betsy warned. "She's got a hooked bill there and a kind of tooth to kill her prey with. We don't want you to be prey!" She laughed as though she had given this talk many times. The word "prey" distracted me as a poet for the moment. Prey. Pray. Was the bird praying for release?

"Let her go! Let her fly!" cried Frankie, distracted from the owls, echoing my thoughts.

"Well, we can't," Miss Betsy responded.

"But look at her flapping! She wants to fly!" The bird did seem to be in a raging need to be set loose.

"This bird has been injured and has lost some crucial feathers. If she tried to fly *even once,* she would fall right down to the earth and die."

"So—fix her!" Frankie said in a demanding voice much like his grandfather Franklin's.

"Sorry, son—she can't be fixed. That's why she's here in the sanctuary."

"Well—where did her feathers go?"

"Some boys shot at her with bb guns. She's happy enough here. She's got other buddies around. Want to see our barn owl? He's a cutie."

"But I want to see *this* bird fly!"

"I'm sorry." She turned to me.

"This bird really does seem to want to leave, though," I said, to show that I was on Frankie's side. And how did she know the bird was *happy enough*? What did that mean? I remember thinking, well of course—*I'm* happy enough.

"Yes. It's in her DNA. She was born to fly. The peregrine falcon is actually the fastest mammal in the world. When she's way up in the sky and spots her prey—just look at those enormous eyes!--, she can plunge at it at a speed of up to two hundred miles an hour. "

"Wow," breathed Frankie. "Like Superman."

"I'll bet you're right. But that one flight would be this bird's last. One dive and--."

"But—but you should be letting her decide for herself!"

What a stupid thing that was for me to say, surely; and yet that imposing bird—she didn't have a crest, but all at once I understood the meaning of the word "crestfallen"-- stared at me once more as though to say, "Honor me. Free me."

So in my dream *I* was the peregrine, deciding whether to plunge just one time and die, or to remain perched and to live a long safe life, denying my nature as a sky-diver in its element. And what decision was I making as that beautiful untamed bird that had forced such a dream upon me?

Well, now I'm *really* awake.

I could go into the living room and read—a light on out there would be way down the hall from the other end of house and Frances' and Frankie's bedrooms—but then I would have to face the Sofa.

A week ago I bought the Sofa on a whim. The one we had was looking a little shabby and, truthfully, I wasn't sure how to clean it, so when I saw this white linen one in the furniture store where I was just passing some idle time, and it had all those cushions, and was on sale (no returns), I pulled out my credit card. Oh, I was in—I said it to myself— "I'm in a buoyant mood for the first time in a year!"-- for some reason that day! I could just picture Franklin lounging on it, and this made me happy.

Yes, to have my husband on this Sofa seemed like a good idea, but as soon as the delivery men set It down yesterday in our living room and promised for an extra twenty dollars to deliver the old one to St. Swithins' thrift shop, I had misgivings.

When I sat on It I had the impression that It was trying to push me off. It was probably my imagination, but It seemed to emit an air of ungratefulness, the same as an unruly protesting toddler I had just saved from marching headlong into the street.

It had been expensive, even on sale. Our house was too prosaic for It, like an impoverished person thinking she could make it through an exclusive girls' academy without the others noticing her and snickering. Ah. That was it: this Sofa was jeering at me, aware of my shame about my upbringing, my early way of life. Our family sofa had been a discarded 1957 Chevy front seat plunked by my Papa into our tiny living room.

I even tried talking to It: "This is Your new home and You are here to stay, Sofa, and I am the boss of You." This was while Frances and Frankie were not in the house. What would they have thought if they had heard me? Or if they thought I was treating It like a sentient being?

The idea of the Sofa perching hunched in my living room now, hulking in the dark, resenting me and my home, makes me grimace.

"It's really pretty, Maya," Frances had told me as she sat back against the cushions and Frankie bounced up and down beside her.

"I am just not sure now—I don't think I like it. Don't bounce, please, Frankie."

"Whoa! My friend Dean-o the Bean-o, his mother lets us *jump* on her couch. With our shoes on!"

My daughter automatically put a restricting hand on her son's arm. "So—take it back." She smoothed the material with her other hand. The Sofa did not resist *her* touch, I noticed.

"Mom—can I make some popcorn? I can make it myself. I know how!"

"Frances, I'm not sure I can return it. It was on sale."

"Oh, Maya, even so—maybe they'd let you exchange it for something else. But I don't know why you don't like it. I know you've have a hard time making up your mind since—you know. I'm proud of you for making a decision."

This is happening more and more often lately. It's not my imagination: Frances is turning into the parent and I into her child. It must have happened after Franklin's disappearance a year ago to this day. Well, sure, I was a mess—what wife wouldn't have been?--, but I did not turn bonkers.

"It's just—Frankie, are your hands clean? Don't *rub* them like that on the armrests!" My eight-year-old grandson scowled and clasped his hands (they did look clean) rebelliously on top of his short sandy-red hair. Frances mimicked him and for a moment they looked like a set of two carrot-topped salt and pepper shakers, sitting innocently enough on this intruder that I have brought into the house.

13

Frankie banged his sneakered heels into the front of the Sofa. Maybe he was also just trying to be the boss of It, but I raised my eyebrows and he stopped. "I like it, too, Maya," he said. "Mo-om, I want popcorn."

I've trained them both to call me Maya. From the time she was an infant Frances was discouraged from calling me "Mama". Frankie has never been allowed to call me "Grandma". Especially since Frances and I have often been told we look more like sisters than mother and daughter.

When I found that Frances was pregnant and she informed me that, "You're about to become a grandmother, Maya!", I went out without even consulting with Franklin and, in a burst of defiance, bought myself a sports car, one too small to fit even a closed-up baby carriage. It didn't matter that Franklin had been teasing Frances for a couple of years, asking when she was going to be a mother—she was only twenty-five and then moved out and away from that dreadful Pete, changing her name legally back to Porter before Frankie was even born, which made me just forty-four, but I wasn't about to admit that to anyone.

Of course I returned the car the next day before Franklin could lecture me.

"Anyway, Frankie, please keep It pristine. I'm maybe going to take It back."

"Whoa! Take it back on your back!" Frankie laughed at his joke. I figured he was picturing me with the damned Thing strapped on me that way, weighed down as I abjectly apologized to the icy salesperson.

"No popcorn, Frankie. I don't want any grease on this sofa, in case I—."

"Maya—it's perfect. Let it be." Frances got up. "Come on, Frank the Tank—popcorn in the family room for you. Want some, Maya?"

"Um-m," I said, studying the Sofa, which sat there in all Its supercilious glory.

I know big words. I am a poet, even though I don't earn a living at it, or choose to, nor have I been able to write anything since Franklin-- left. I may have come from a rural area ("Big hearts, empty pockets" Franklin used to say about us people from West Virginia, showing his ignorance of those of us he had to live with), but I still had access in high school to a Thesaurus! I won it in a poetry contest. I still have it. It's my most prized book.

If I could only write a poem! I'm sure that would ease me. But my skills this past year have dumbed down to a single ditty:

My Franklin lies over the ocean/ My Franklin lies over the sea,

My Franklin lies over the ocean/ Oh bring back my Franklin to me.

Bring back, oh bring back, oh bring back my Franklin to me-e-e-!

Bring back, oh bring back, oh bring back my Franklin to me.

You know how when you have a song in your head that just won't go away? There it is. I never sing it so that anyone can hear it, especially Frances and Frankie, but I catch myself humming it every now and then.

(I have no nest but a cage now, metal-gray like yours. No room to spread my wings. Nightly I worry my tethers. The cording carries the rank odor of my captors. A fresh kill smells kinder than this prison.)

I sit up in bed. I can't be afraid to go into my own living room. I must do this, maybe sleep for the rest of the night *on* the Sofa and let It know once and for all that I am boss.

But what if I wrinkle or stain It somehow? What if I fall asleep and drool on It and the store won't take It back? It is the elephant

16

in my house. It has made no effort to become my friend, to adjust to Its new living quarters. I would like to hear something like a sigh of relief from It, to have It be even slightly grateful for having found Its home; but no, It just takes up space and broods, causing *me* to act like the outsider in my own home.

I leave my glasses on that I never let anyone see me wear, not even Franklin. Using the light from my cellphone, I enter the living room from the master bedroom. I can hear no sound from the far end of the house—lucky family, deep in sleep!—and I turn on a light beside the Sofa, careful not to touch It.

Buoyant, I had been in such a buoyant mood!-- and I suck in my breath, because it hits me with a jolt that the *cushions* look buoyant, as though if Franklin had them he would float ashore on them and be safe.

Agh-h! A spasm of grief passes through me. What craziness! So I actually bought It for *him,* not for *me.* Unconsciously I must have known that it was a year since I saw him last and was still waiting for him to come home and what a wonderful surprise I would have for him with a new sofa!

I sit down in Franklin's imported leather chair that still smells vaguely of his special cologne. I stare across the room at the Sofa, and I cry as quietly as I can, holding my hands over my mouth—I cry for Franklin, for myself, for *just not knowing.* I don't dare hug one of those two perky pillows that came with the Sofa, because what if I dampened It with my tears and I couldn't return It?

Oh, where *are* you, Franklin? Damn it, where *are* you? People in official uniforms brought your foam cooler to the house after they'd peeled the duct tape away looking for clues; and here was your ancient tape recorder inside, the one you had had me speak into all those years ago. Notes in your own voice for Frances; and both insulting and loving last words for me. Did you know you were dying? Did you die before your boat caught fire and exploded? Did you die before a shark got to you?

Stop it, Maya. *Stop*. No. I refuse to believe you are gone. None of that is possible. Therefore, Franklin, you are still alive and you will walk through our front door any day now and it will be like something out of a soap opera with your having had amnesia for the past year—people do that, don't they—have amnesia? And you will return because you just remembered that you have a wife and a daughter and a grandson who love you and need you and you will fall onto that Sofa, still in your clothes wet from the Atlantic Ocean, maybe with seaweed in your hair, fall onto It in relief and you will laugh, "Maya—you made a decision! What a wonderful woman!"

I hate that Sofa.

Two.
Mayetta Jane McDowell, age 18
summer, 1985 Jerome, West Virginia

<u>I Planted This Tree</u>   a poem by Maya Porter   undated

I planted this tree. It became mine when I chose it,

Bought it, brought it

Home. Tended, watered, fed it. My tree

Came as high as my knee.

A bottle-brush, well-named. I guess it lured

A hummingbird

Or two. I never was alert enough

To catch them there. My tree grew until

I had to tilt my head back to view its crown.

The point is this: I knew this about my tree. I knew

What it would look like as it sang toward the sky.

I planted a child (no, not alone):

Nurtured her, tended her, watered and fed until

I had to tilt my head back

As she sang toward the sky.

The point is this: I knew my tree's future,

Knew what to expect. So here's the conundrum,

The miracle: rooted, watered, fed, this child

(Some like me, some like him), grew to be

Her own.

*   *   *

"Make up your mind!"

I recall ten years ago how my Momma stood, hands on her hips, a look of exasperation on her face ("I am gettin' *exasperated* with you, Mayetta Jane!") while I shifted my eight-year-old body from one skinny leg to the other, caught between two choices that both seemed equally good (or bad) to me.

"What's the third choice?" I said, hopin' to get a smile from her. If I could make her laugh I would be home free. 'Course I earned a slap 'stead of a laugh. But you never know.

I learnt this from Momma and how she could maybe make Papa laugh instead of him hittin' her.

Trouble makin' up my mind. And when I discovered poems and *then* discovered I had a gift for writin' 'em, suddenly there was another ongoing problem—pickin' one word over another when they both seemed like the right one.

My poems, the poems I write that are gonna get me in college this fall on a scholarship and I not only will get to be the first in my family to graduate from college—I will be the first of all my relatives to graduate from *high school* here in Jerome!—My teacher says there's power in words and she's right. I can be as funny as I want and get back at people, too, in my poems, and look all innocent at the same time—like the time when we read about King Arthur and I had a revelation: I didn't want to be the queen or anything like that; no, oh boy, what I wanted to be was the *court jester*.

And then I read this poem by A.A. Milne about a sailor who couldn't make up his mind and it was like he was writin' just to me, like he knew me and we was both laughin' together about how funny life is and I cried out loud, "Oh Lord, *I want to write like this, too!*"

Now gone to trash. Just gone to trash. My whole entire life back to ze-ro. And I have totally lost my sense of humor. Bein' a kinda jester won't get me out of this. Laughin' about it won't turn my body around. This one impulsive act of lettin' somebody else make a decision for me has driven my fierceness right outa me!

Oh Lordy. What if I'm pregnant? I never did this with a man before. Red don't even believe me, but it's true.

I am so scared that I'm pregnant. Oh, why did I have to be so uppity about sittin' in the classroom all the time writin' my poems? I could of hung around the girls room and the lockers while the girls was changin' into their gym shorts, and listened to 'em talk about their bodies and how to keep boys away without makin' 'em mad. Those kinds of particulars girls shared with each other, not their mommas—things like if you set your mind on Jesus while you were makin' out, it was okay then and not a sin. Sure, I was curious about the actual gettin' together—Momma told me I'd find out about stuff when the time was right, and sure I knew about what our hens and rooster did, and I'd seen goats climb on each other, kind of the way Red just now did with me— but they never seemed to think it hurt, and Momma said they knew when it was their season and they always got pregnant right after.

What if it's *my* season? I know my time of the month was a coupla weeks ago, but Momma says I'm "irregular" and I don't dare ask her what that means, except I gotta be careful and carry a "that time of month" pad with me all the time, and a couple of pins, just in case.

I'm scared to tell anybody. Especially my guidance counselor lady and my English teacher. They'll take away my scholarship. But I need it for college. Even community college costs money. Nobody in my family's even made it through high school, so what do they know about *college*? I'm s'posed to start next month, and *I* don't even know what it's like.

But I got to tell somebody! I'm goin' to hell for sure. Is the girl supposed to be in charge of these things? I heard of a girl right down the road from us and she told her Momma, and her Daddy kicked her out of the house. Right out. No time to pack or nothin'.

How did I ever let Red do that to me?

I thought it was s'posed to be beautiful, but all it did was hurt and then he was risin' over me and rollin' off. No sound in our West Virginia woods except for my gaspin' from the sudden pain and his heavy breathin', the kind I was used to hearin' from my Papa and Momma's bedroom when I would get up from cramps and roam the house in the middle of the night. The sound was an ugly not-human one and once more as I edged my way back to my bed in the dark I would vow to only give myself to a man who truly, passionately, to-the-death loved me.

For some reason the memory of that nighttime breathin' made me hate Red for a moment.

Then, right outta the blue, I wrote a poem in my head:

"He loves me as the knights of yore/

Who said before they went to war/

I'll think of you forever, dear/

And cherish all our moments here."

And that was right off the top of my head! That was *good!*

"That was good!" I said out loud, so proud of myself.

"Good, huh?" Red said. I nodded, concentratin' on composin' my poem in my head. "Compared to who?" he demanded.

I had no idea what he was talkin' about. Red— that's just his nickname. His real one is Michael Patrick Murphy—he's my knight in shining armor. I've been too shy to tell him so, though. I really wanted to get to a piece of paper and a pencil so's I could write down my poem before I forgot it. I do better with paper and pencil than with my memory.

"Well, *you* sure were good." I recall he ordered me to brush the leaves off his back. It had rained the night before and the still-wet oak and chestnut leaves were makin' a kind of pattern on his sunburnt freckled back. I guess the Irish always get sunburnt 'stead of tan. Red sure has a lot of freckles to go with that carrot-head of hair.

I didn't tell him what I call his hair, but I wrote a poem about it when I was cow-eyed back in the spring watchin' him play baseball, back when we first started datin'. It started: "When I'm in bed/I dream of red/ Not gold or green or blue"--.

"What—what do we do now? Red? What if I'm-- pregnant?"

"You're not. I was careful. But so what? So we'll get married. We was gonna, anyway."

"Sure. After I finish college." I just wanted to sing those words with a kind of joy: *I. Finish. College.*

I recall that Red snorted and frowned. "You're kiddin', right? College for you and then what? They gonna teach you how to be an Army wife to me?"

I pulled myself up and went behind the biggest chestnut tree I could find. Shy now, I shook myself so Red couldn't see me. But he was lyin' back down and shadin' his eyes from the sunlight that sprinkled itself through the branches. His underwear was gray and I had a flash of feelin' better than his Momma, because *I* would know how to keep those underthings whiter than that in the washtub. She still made her own soap, I guessed. What a stubborn woman.

Birds chirped at me from up in the trees. There was no other sound.

Miss Pendleton said my poetry had promise. She's the one found me the scholarship. And now I was gonna to let her down, and Momma—maybe if I could *shake* myself hard enough I could shake all the stuff outta me that Red had just put in.

But my hand, when I ran it up my leg, came away sticky. Maybe it was stickin' inside of me right this minute, turnin' into a baby! I knew a girl once jumped off the mountainside up South Pass Road. She broke both legs and *still* had her baby.

Momma said when you got married and had a husband you was stuck. Maybe this was what she was talkin' about. Maybe this was the price of sin. Oh, why hadn't I been concentratin' on *Jesus*? My face got hot, thinkin' of the pastor thunderin' at me over his pulpit, pointin' his finger at me, Mayetta Jane McDowell, while my Momma cringed in horror and my Papa clenched his fist at me and Red.

Red had it easy. He could do what he wanted and then go to confession at his Catholic Church and then go out and do whatever he wanted to again.

I didn't want to be stuck, havin' babies and waitin' for Red to come home at night or maybe from another part of the world in his Army uniform. I didn't want to be—*tamed*, like Momma.

I couldn't tell Miss Pendleton. I couldn't bear seein' her face, how I'd just let her down. Would they put my name on a list of "NEVER GIVE MAYETTA JANE McDOWELL NO MORE MONEY FOR COLLEGE"? I didn't want a baby! I wanted to go to school some more and end up in someplace pretty, with a good job. Greenville. Now that had to be a pretty name for a place to live and work.

Oh, how had I let him talk me into doin' this?

"Uh uh, Red. I can't decide," I had said kinda shyly, hopin' he'd back off and stop pesterin' me, but he said, "Never mind. Just you let me do the decidin' for the two of us," and here we were. . . .

So when Red left me at my house and he loped off to his job at Walmart, with me bein' terrified that he was goin' to brag to his friends what we had done-- I got up the courage and told Momma-- Momma, who had her arms in soapy water at the sink, who slapped me across the face with a wet sudsy hand so that I tasted blood and Ivory soap and chlorine, and who then told me to shut up. I was too shocked to cry, anyway.

"Sit down, Mayetta Jane." I sat and made my expression a stony one—I wasn't goin' to let her see me cry-- and faced her across our chipped green metal kitchen table. It was a big thing when she used my whole name, which I hated. It sounded so—country and backwoods. I wanted to change mine to somethin' romantic like Sara or Emily or Edna, my favorite poets.

"Now you look at me and you pay attention, Mayetta. We gotta think. What was goin' on in your head, girl? Red's not ever gonna amount to anythin'." She pushed back her hair, leavin' some soap in it and makin' it stand up some; and I noticed again how gray she was gettin'.

"He's ok," I murmured. I recalled to myself how full of life he'd looked to me on the outdoor basketball court, chargin' back and forth and ignorin' the whistle, searchin' for me—me!—on the sidelines and the other girls in my class starin' at me hard in burnin'-up-honest-to-God jealousy.

"He's a bum and he's gonna get in the Army and find hisself some drugs and he'll end up dead like his Daddy. That what you want?"

I didn't know why I felt the need to defend Red. "Well—he said we'll get married."

She raised her wet reddened hand to me again and then dropped it. She'd been wringin' out wet clothes when I told her I thought I could be pregnant. I was lucky she hadn't slapped me across the face with one of them soakin' wet towels. When they're wrung out they got a kick like a fibery rope.

28

(Could "fibery" be a word? I'd have to ask Miss Pendleton. Or I could check my Thesaurus.)

"Hey—we're talkin' about your future, missy. Pay attention. He use any protection?" she asked, her eyes narrowed. I winced. Actually, the memory of that thing of his stickin' up like that, like it had a life of its own, so white with the rest of his body so much darker, had made me shut my eyes.

"I—I don't know. I mean, it all happened so fast." I have to admit I was feelin' relief now at tellin' her. She was mad, sure, but at least she wasn't turnin' me out of the house. I knew a girl once—

Was she gonna hit me again? If she did I just knew I was gonna start blubberin'. She was starin' up towards the ceilin' now, her eyes all of a sudden wide, her arms grippin' the kitchen table so that gray sudsy water dripped down off her elbows.

"Mayetta--you remember what Pastor said just last Sunday?"

I strained to recall, but all I could see in my mind's eye in our little Methodist Church was Red's grin. Lordy, that seemed like a lifetime ago.

"He said that all things work to the good for those who love the Lord."

"Saint Paul said that one." I was proud of my Bible-learnin'.

"We don't have time for your sass, Mayetta Jane."

"Sorry." The thunder had left Momma's face, at least. She was gonna help me!

"Okay. Listen up, now. Maybe this is God's way of clearin' a path, showin' us—so we gotta look at this as a opportunity. Now here's what we're gonna do." We both sat at the kitchen table, our palms cuppin' our chins, across from each other like book ends. We were so alike! Blonde hair, sky-blue eyes, kinda slopin' shoulders unless we stood up tall. Me just a inch taller than her, but not ever willin' to chance teasin' her about it. I could look at her and see what I would look like when I got older, and believe you me, I was not enjoyin' the view. Look at all the gray in her hair, and the worn-away hands. I couldn't look at her hands without wantin' to cry.

"You gotta sleep with Mr. Franklin."

I gawped at her. "That's crazy! I can't do that!"

"Yes, you can and you will, too. Good things can come from bad, and this is your way outta this town. Don't you give me that look, Mayetta! The Lord just put this inta my head, so you listen. I seen Mr. Franklin notice you at his diggin' site. You're the best-lookin' thing this town of Jerome has to offer—don't you blush! You know it's true, and any fool with eyes in his head knows it too, includin' him."

"No! That's awful! I can't do that! *I won't!* What kinda solution is that?"

"Yes, you will. You're gonna. If you're havin' a child, it's gonna be his and not that Irish shit Red's. His fam'ly was never no good. Why you *ever* let yourself--"

"But, Momma--no! Not Mr. Franklin! He's—old!"

Mr. Franklin Porter, Junior, age 25, was sent here in his BMW by his big bucks daddy to start a mill plant with some kinda gov'ment grant. He was like that poem Miss Pendleton had read us in class: "He glittered when he walked." The endin' of that poem wasn't so upliftin', but I still thought of it as describin' Mr. Franklin. He looked like he must smell good up close.

I was aware, but didn't want Momma to know that I knew, that Mr. Franklin watched me. When he was talkin' to the high school principal and I would come by (and I made sure I came by pretty slowlike down the hall, kinda practicin' how I would amble up to Red), he would stop talkin' and he would make a little nod in my direction. I would smile—I had good teeth—"No braces needed for you, young lady," the visitin' dentist would say when we all lined up at school—as though anybody in our school'd be able to pay for braces like a Hollywood movie star!—and I would smile, proud of my nice straight teeth. Mr. Franklin was like a movie star his own self, tall and dark-headed and so clean—you jest knew *his* underwear was white; maybe *he'd* had braces, 'cause his teeth were so nice.

I'd watched. Oh, I'd watched. I was flattered in a funny way, kinda boastful way. He didn't seem to be payin' attention to anybody much 'cept me.

"Make up your mind, Mayetta. And you can't wait long. You don't want no six-month baby that weighs ten pounds."

"That's all crazy, Momma! What about college? And my scholarships?"

"Shoulda been thinkin' about those when you went moonin' after Mr. Red."

"Well, I won't do it!" And I ran outside to sit on the back stoop and cry 'til my eyes was as red as my boyfriend's hair.

Of course my body didn't care how miserable I was. I finally had to stop cryin' before Papa got home and I hurt the baby somehow with my sobbin'. Oh, I was frantic, tryin' to come up with a better plan than Momma's! I knew I was goin' straight to hell!

But then in the middle of the night with Momma's thinkin' in mind I started to figure maybe I *wouldn't* be goin' to hell, if it was okay with Saint Paul and it was in the Bible. Even people in the Old Testament had done this kinda thing and even King David had brought right from wrong in his doin's with Bathsheba . I fretted that like David's, this baby would be born and then God would make it die. I didn't want that to happen to someone so young and innocent, even though I kept prayin' mightily that I wasn't expectin'.

Then I figured that if that kinda awful disaster happened when I give birth, why then!-- it would be a sign from God that I could just walk away from Mr. Franklin and wait for Red to get out of the Army.

And if it was born and looked just like Red—why, then, I'd up and tell Mr. Franklin that he wasn't the Daddy nohow and I was leavin' him and takin' the baby with me, right into the Army with Red. And Mr. Franklin would be all calm and polite about this and he would promise to give me money for the baby and me, enough so's I could hire a babysitter and go to college.

That was it! And I'd worked it out myself. I wouldn't tell Momma, but this sure seemed like a good plan. And at the end of it was Red.

O Absalom, O Absalom! I didn't quite remember what that little chant meant in my head, but it sounded like a poem or a prayer. And I knew it was from the Bible.

Of course I hadn't thought of this no-fail plan yet while Momma was talking at me. I wasn't about to share it with her, neither. "But what if Mr. Franklin doesn't like me, Momma?"

Momma had snorted. "I'm gettin' exasperated with you, Mayetta. Didn't I teach you 'bout men?"

"No! You told me it was better, me not knowin', so's I wouldn't go out tryin' that stuff."

"Yeah. Well, now's your chance. You seen animals ruttin'? Well, then—men are just like animals," And then she told me about the lusts of men and how women had to be the guardians of civilization. I wanted to stopper up my ears when she got more detailed, but at least it explained Red hurryin' through what he had done.

In the end it was easier than I figured. I moseyed over to Mr. Franklin's little office at the construction site and I asked him what did he think of the community college at Ford Creek, two towns over? I told him I had a scholarship, which was a bald-faced lie. I didn't have it yet, 'cept I had my fingers crossed behind my back; and I asked him did he think a girl could make it through, workin' and studyin' at the same time, because I sure did want to make somethin' of myself. I wasn't lyin' about that part. There was some kinda wild fiery hot poker of a backbone to me, just like to my Momma—except mine melted when Red was around.

"Mr. Franklin, you ever been to Greenville?"

"Which one?" he asked, lookin' down at me, his hands in his pockets. His leather boots were so clean! How did he do that in all this dust?

"What? Is there more than the one?"

He laughed, but I could tell it wasn't *at* me. "Just call me Franklin," he said, and takin' his hands out free, he shook my right hand. His nails was clean and so better-lookin' than mine that I tried to pull my hand away, I was so embarrassed; but he held on a little longer than I thought proper, which made me recall Momma's words about men in general and this got my hopes up.

We rode in Franklin's car (I'd never smelled a smell like this—he said it was leather, and I told him I'd have to write a poem about how cows outside in the fields didn't smell this good, and he laughed—I could make him laugh!) to the movie house in Ford Creek and on the way I pointed out the college, proud as if I was already goin' there.

He talked a lot in his funny accent—I guess he was lonely, bein' far from his home up north in Boston. He told me how he wanted to succeed at this buildin' job he had, because then his Daddy would find him some better places to go. Then he apologized 'cause he knew it was my home town, but I was thinkin', I guess it doesn't matter where you come from; a Daddy always wants you to do good. Then I felt a cold shudder of time runnin' out—if he moved away too soon it would be just me and Red and the baby. And an unforgivin' Momma. Not to mention Papa--!

"Uh—Franklin—could ya drive a little slower, please?"

He glanced over at me. I was holdin' onto the door handle and he was careenin' around the curves like he knew where he was goin' and like there wasn't nobody else on the road. I was feelin' green and all too aware that I was most likely carryin' Red's child.

"You don't have to worry. I know how to drive," he said, kind of like he was defensive about it.

"I know, I know. But I think I et somethin' that kinda upset my stomach and I'm kinda worried about the insides of your nice car—."

He slowed down.

When I felt some better I told him a little about my poems and I forgot for the moment what Momma had told me I had to do with him, and do it fast, and here's the real surprise—I kinda felt warm toward him. He smelled like he'd got washed just for our date and that touched me. He was all smiley-eyed and gentle, nothin' like that big showoff Red and—now this had nothin' to do with Momma's and my plans, but it was somethin' that wormed into my brain and wouldn't let go.

And then—now this was *my* idea, mine alone, and it come at me like God Hisself was commandin' me, it was such a powerful idea! So I confessed with my face kinda turned away from him, I was that shy about askin' for favors, that I wanted to talk like him and would he correct me and get me talkin' better-- like him?

He was havin' coffee after the movie and I was slurpin' down an ice cream float and we was laughin' 'cause the freezin' cold ice cream was givin' me hiccups and I was blushin'.

He stopped all of a sudden and really, I mean *really* looked at me like I never been looked at before. I jest sat still as I could, tryin' not to burp.

"Where has an angel like you come from?" he asked. I blushed, but only 'cause he was leanin' in so close.

"I mean it. You are just drop-dead, all-out gorgeous. I can't stop staring at you and I know it's impolite, but if I could bottle that kind of beauty and sell it I would be a millionaire."

I had only an inklin' what he was talkin' about. People had been tellin' me how pretty I was since I was a baby and Papa had been threatenin' to take it outta my hide and I had heard "pride goeth before a fall" from Momma jest as soon as I could tell her voice from anyone else's, so I jest waited.

"You really want my help, Maya?"

Maya. Oh, listen to that—he made it sound like music.

I had jest decided on that name—Mr. Franklin was the first person I said it out loud to-- and hearin' him say it to me made me glow and lower my head. If folks could be born again, couldn't they have a new name again? Once I knew a girl changed her name and she wasn't getting' married or anythin'. Just didn't like her name. Her Daddy'd named her Daisy Mae—imagine!—and she went and changed it to Shelley, like the movie actress Shelley Winters who gained a lotta weight, but they still kep' her in the movies. It was the last thing Daisy told me she did before she ran away. I wish I knew what happened to her.

I nodded. "Yes. I promise."

"All right. Tell you what--I'll be your 'enry 'iggins and you'll be my Eliza."

"Doolittle," I said, so proud of myself. I knew what he was talkin' about. I'd seen that movie once on our little tv. I grew bolder when he grinned. "What's the first thing-- Franklin?" Another hiccup. I covered my mouth.

"Okay." He hesitated. "Although the task appears Herculean."

I frowned, not understanding. He noticed. "My apologies. All right. For starters—how about, when you have a word that ends in 'ing', you pronounce the 'g'?"

"I—don't get what you're talkin' about--"

"There's one. Say 'talking', instead of 'talkin'."

"Talk-ing," I said. "Don't I say that already?"

"Well. Well. I'll tell you what." He got up, so I did, too. He pulled out the most luxurious wallet I had ever seen in my life. I had wanted to finish the rest of my soda, but that was a kid thing and I needed not to do kid things right now in front of Franklin. "I have a tape recorder back at my place. We'll go get it and you can listen to yourself. Ever done that?" I shook my head. He paused. "You're really certain you want to do this?"

"If you got the time. Yes. Yes. Yes. Make me talk like you." I actually was excited about this, doin' somethin'—*doing something* for myself and at the same time doin' somethin' to get in good with Franklin.

I admit I even wanted to brag to him about comin' in first place in the poetry contest and winnin' my Thesaurus, so I tried my new word on him: "Franklin, that is really a luxurious-lookin'— looking wallet." He grinned at that and ran his hands through his thick brown hair.

That night *I* ran my hands through that hair and we made love. It's gonna be his baby, I thought. No. It's *going* to be his baby. Red had done kinda—kind of—*bullying* sex, but this was different, somehow.

Was Franklin in love with me or did he marry me out of duty, when I told him I was pregnant? Only Momma witnessed our wedding. His papa and mine refused to attend and it wasn't until many years later, after Franklin had made his own fortune, that he told me his papa had cut him off with only a dollar, to show that Franklin, Senior meant it.

I stopped worrying that I was goin'—*going*-- to hell for deceiving my new husband.

Red stomped off into the military after cussin' –cussing me out and threatenin'—threatening to beat me.

"Try it and I'll report you to the Army and they'll never in a million years take you and that's *after* they lock you up," I said right straight to his face, surprisin' myself-- and even *that* didn't make him back off until his buddies came running and pulled him offa me.

Franklin's and my only child, Frances, was born when I was 19 and Franklin 26 and she would be his joy, his delight, his grin all wobbly when he picked her up and held her—"Maya, put down that pencil and come look at her hair. What do you think—all those curls and such a sandy-reddish color. Rather a mixture of yours and mine, I guess. Frances, my precious. You look like a Southie. My father would have a fit." (I didn't know that was a Boston place and I gulped, fearing he was talking about Red.)

"You're beautiful, anyway, my little darlin'," he would coo to her and then I would laugh, hearing him drop his 'g'.

After I got her nursed and down to nap I would think about writing some more poems, but I was so tired and she was so fretful that my brain felt like mush. I did write:

"My brain is foggy

My blouse is soggy

My voice is froggy

Go to sleep, baby—please go to sleep."

That was the best I could do for a long time. I never did write a poem about Franklin. I'm sorry about that now.

Three.

Franklin   early fall, 1985   Jerome, West Virginia

I consider that I played my cards wrong, so wrong.

At first.

Even after all my frantic calls to Father about how I hated this town and how people would rather drink or drug themselves up on pills, telling their country bumpkin doctor that they had some undefined medical condition, and laying it on Father how this was such a lost cause, he still abandoned me—dumped me here!

I wanted to be back in civilized Boston with Phyllis. It kept looking less and less likely that she'd come join me here after she finished law school at Harvard and received her degree. I knew these people in Jerome didn't need lawyers. They needed a good high school.

"Franklin," she'd said the last time I saw her (she'd insisted on choosing the Boston hotel where she couldn't possibly be sighted by her classmates, and then against all odds ran into two of them at the front desk and with true New England politeness we all nodded and looked the other way as if to agree not to mention this again), "here's the long and short of it." And then the damned woman had the temerity to tell me that she'd accepted a position in Washington, D.C. She named the firm and even I had to be impressed. Her parents must have arranged something. They both knew how to pull strings. I hated to admit they were even better at it than my own father.

"Washington's not all that far from West Virginia," she argued just as smoothly as a silky defense attorney as she pinned up her platinum hair into a kind of bun at the nape of the neck I'd been biting on so short a time ago. I watched her, hungry for more delicious skin time with her, but I knew the signal that we were through for the night was when she pinned up her hair.

She turned and studied me. "I have to get back to my books, Franklin."

"So you want to leave me here by myself? May I please remind you how much this room cost? And we only used one bed."

"You're losing your charm. I thought Southern gentlemen had better manners."

She pulled me up into a sitting position and kissed me, her beautiful fingers clenching my upper arms. "Oh, those muscles. Not fair that you're tall and good-looking and you have that remarkable body."

"Remind me to show you all my swimming trophies someday when you're in my bedroom. "

"Not if it's in West Virginia, Franklin."

"I don't know what the hell West Virginia is! It doesn't feel like the South, it's doesn't act like the North, it—it can go to blazes!"

"So go back to your father and have him give you another assignment."

"Cool as cucumbers, aren't you?"

"That a West Virginia saying? Don't try to corner me, Franklin. Look, tell you what—as soon as I'm settled in the D.C. area—"

"No! That's going to be months from now!"

"—as soon as I'm settled, I'll come to you. Maybe we can meet in the middle, someplace in Virginia—"

I looked at her perfect body and pictured her behind a desk in Washington, laughing with all the conquest-hungry upward-mobile lawyers who worked out all the time and bleached their teeth. I didn't like that picture, so, irked as I was, I pictured her dead, that gorgeous body jammed into a trashcan behind the hotel, the bun de-pinned, the hair splayed out against her bare shoulders. Those gorgeous shoulders now set sternly against me.

"Franklin, for God's sake quit sulking. You're too handsome to pull it off." And just like that, she was gone.

I had sufficient time that night after I decided which bed to use (the one that still smelled like us or the virginal one? I finally collapsed, drunk, on the unmade one) to ask myself if my father was doing this on purpose to punish me. Was he serious about building a textile plant in Jerome, West Virginia, or was it something I'd done? Was this just a tax break for him? Once more I wished Mother was still alive to rein him in. She'd never have allowed her only child to languish in *any* hell hole. Oh, she'd been so much fun, rest her indecorous bones.

Was he tired of losing money on his son? Was this the punishment then? "Franklin, I am through paying for colleges you don't finish. My colleagues are making jokes about what school are you attending this week and what is your latest major."

Hence Jerome, West Virginia, and no fooling around this time. Father was serious about cutting off any kind of allowance-slash-paycheck.

And then just three weeks later Phyllis did the worst, lowest thing possible to me—she wrote me that she had finally admitted to herself that she was gay and was moving in with her lover DeNeece. How could women do such a thing? Was she joking with me? Was this just an excuse to let me down easily?

Wasn't I a man?

Enter Maya, who seemed both shy and eager to be with me. Sure I'd made that joke about Dr. Higgins and Eliza Doolittle; but the way she wrapped her tasty long legs around me! Was this what these backwoods babes did for entertainment when the tv reception went haywire in these mountains?

45

Actually. . .this could do while I got over Phyllis (maybe I'd send that bitch a letter and call her 'Phil'—"Which one of you is the guy?" I'd write) and in the meantime Maya was proving to be a very quick learner.

It was almost fun to teach her. I know myself and I know that I need to amuse myself. All work and no play makes Franklin quite obnoxious. I know that about me. I work best when there's a reward, and not at the *end* of the work, either. I like rewards all the way through the laborious parts. Perhaps this is what is meant by "comic relief". I know that when Maya and I were not making love I found her rather laughable.

Maybe I could become an English instructor. Except not here in Jerome, this place small enough that people were already giving me proprietary, territorial looks. I wasn't sure if these hillbillies would trash my BMW while I wasn't around. Maya was good at not looking possessive when we were together, but still—.

Then she told me she was pregnant.

All right. I have plenty of ambition when I choose. Just not for this damned construction kind of job forced onto me by my father. And I counted on his helping us out when I phoned him and told him, no, I would not make her get an abortion, even if it was legal here—actually we could all go to jail for even *thinking* about it among all the God-damned evangelical Christians here in Jerome--that I was going to do the right thing by her. And no, of course it wasn't some other man's! If my father could only see her face he'd realize what a tractable, willing helpmate-in-the-rough Maya was (although to myself I'd already decided that I'd drop her fast if she didn't measure up and if she wasn't actually expecting), and for the first time in my easygoing life I was going to stand up and be a man, a man with—with—values and moreover. . . .

But my father (translate to "cash cow") had hung up and disinherited me long before I got to the word he so longed for in me.

Values.

"I'm sorry, Franklin," Maya told me.

"Hm-m?"

"That was a mean thing your Daddy did, just leavin'—"

"Leaving," I corrected her automatically.

"Leaving. Right, Franklin? Leav-ing. Listen-ing. Lov-ing. I love you, Franklin. Wait—I am loving you, Franklin. Even with that cute Boston accent you got!"

I would have said, "You 'have', not 'got'," but I'd stopped paying attention to her. I'd been working on her to lower her voice and to get the twang out of it, but actually I had just this moment discovered something about myself! I, Franklin Porter, Jr., just having been disinherited and also brushed off by a nouveau lesbian and about to become a father myself, realized a potential I had not heretofore unearthed in myself and was now holding in my mind like a rare gem, turning it this way and that, not quite believing my find and reveling in it: *I didn't enjoy construction.* Rather:

I enjoyed finding and persuading people with money who enjoyed construction!

And to do that I had to get us out of Jerome, West Virginia.

Long story short: that's how we came to Durham, North Carolina (where I knew a slick college buddy and where God's gift from Heaven itself, my angelic Frances was born. Wouldn't Father fall in love with her when he finally met her, and meet her he must) and then to Raleigh (on a great, just slightly illegal tip from the buddy's buddy). From there west to Winston-Salem, enticing moneyed prospects at every stop while Maya grumbled about when were we going to set up housekeeping on a permanent basis—"I want it as soon as possible. How can the child settle down in one place if you're uprooting us all the time, Franklin?" Then south to Charlotte and then Columbia, South Carolina, my moving us from one rental to another with my newly tapped unerring intuition, to Orlando to make some large fast money off the Disney-come-latelys.

And then—then the *whining* from my Eliza Doolittle of a wife who'd fast enough become used to hairdressers, manicures, babysitters, evenings out in new outfits, so scared that people would see her for what she was, an outsider, covering over her

48

insecurities with my money ("I jest want to be in a nice quiet little town!"—that from Maya; "Quiet? Or dead like Jerome, where you hardly had electricity in your house?" I would counter), looking at which direction Orlando would overflow to and guessing wrong for the first time as I reached for millionaire status—not a long reach, given those days—take *that*, Father!) to a place on the Atlantic east coast, to a drowsy town south of Cocoa Beach, one with its own airport, thanks to its proximity to the Cape, so that I could come and go when I pleased, even to Phyllis in D.C., who had tired (as I guessed she would) of her lesbian status (and who had learned some terrific new moves in bed—who knew?), a town that I knew Maya would fit into, given her degree of recently acquired sophistication, a town where I could be as big a frog as I wanted, a town I could awaken with enough Other People's Money: Banana Bay, Florida.

Four.

Franklin May 17, 2018 Atlantic Ocean, a few miles off Banana Bay Beach

Will my old tape recorder stay dry? When I'm through talking into it I'm going to remove the batteries to lighten its weight, wrap it in a plastic waterproof sheet, tape it securely, place it into this Styrofoam fishing chest I brought along, and seal the whole thing with duct tape. If this works, I'm going to wish that I'd invested in duct tape.

It will be my last record of who I am/was. It would seem as though, the way this boat is taking on water, that I'm fairly close to being drowned. Busybodies will wonder why I bought a used one instead of a new one, which I damn well could have afforded. Good. They need their unexamined lives shaken up. Truth is that I was attracted to the history of this one and how it had been used to smuggle drugs a while back. A boat with a past. Just call me a romantic s.o.b.

Different story if I'd waited two weeks—then there would be a full moon. As it is, I've only got a sliver of one to navigate by. Just past the new moon and only some 3% visible. That's either good news or bad news, depending on if you want to see the sharks coming or not. But that's all water over the dam, to coin a phrase. Johnstown Flood. Funny what trivia the mind retains, even in times of crisis.

 At least there are stars.

Oh, Frances, Frances, my beloved daughter, the light and love of my life! Be good to my grandson. I never got a chance to christen this boat with your name, more's the pity. You would have loved it. Franklin II--tell him—tell little "Frank The Tank" I loved him. I wish now I'd bought him a dog. But *I* never had one, so. . . well, regrets, regrets. And someone may have heard my weak Mayday before the transmission regretfully sputtered and died, so I could be just moments away from being rescued. That would certainly alter what's going on.

Frances--take care of your mother. You *need* to, Frances, because—because I got your mother used to money and I got her used to thinking that she had to pretend she was from anywhere else than her hardscrabble roots in West Virginia—yes, I know she never let on to you in all these years that she was from there and she's probably shrieking bloody blue murder listening to this now that, as they say in Boston, the cat's out of the bag--, anyway, that was wrong of me and seems so trivial now, but it was an easy cheap way to get her to shut up. Actually there was nothing she actually had to apologize for—(the lights in this damned cabin are starting to dim—I have to hurry)—but it was easy to unsettle her, because you see, it was simply like just a game, the kind Mother and I used to play, a game to me and before you even came along, I had gotten her used to— Frances, I swear to you your mother before I met her had never once deceived anyone *in her life!* Read her poems. You see how innocent they were, those early ones that she wrote. It's simply not in her nature.

No. *I* was the one who got Maya hooked on *deception. She* was the one already trained in not being able to make up her mind about anything. Too eager to please others before taking care of herself. I never could teach her the art of selfishness.

Oh. That's a book, by the way. Probably out of print now. The Art of Selfishness. And it *is* an art.

Hey, Trump, ever read that book? Ever read *any* book? I think it's a tasty irony that, the same day I'm shoveling water out of this leaky sieve of a boat, he's reported on this little just-died tv in the cabin here, to have given $130,000 to Michael Cohen-- and Trump denies it-- for that looker Stormy Daniels. C'mon, T.— those who already believe you can do no wrong are following you like obedient lemmings, and those of us who wonder how a dipshit like you made it into the same office where Lincoln used to sit are just waiting for you to get hit in the head by an errant golf ball.

Then *that's* followed on tv by this congressman from Alabama who states about climate change that "Every time you have that soil or rock, whatever it is, that is deposited into the seas, *that* forces the water levels to rise."

I will be glad to leave these bozos to their own nimrod ways. If I were not a Boston Brahmin born and bred I would be pounding on the door of my taxicab and yelling in a Bronx accent, "Whaddaya, *nuts*?"

It is a fruitless exercise indeed to be going to one's demise pondering politics.

There is this thing about time. I ponder it often. Right now seems like a good reason to wax philosophical, with my feet sloshing in cold green salt water.

Well, pay attention. Here it is, anyway: there has to be a microsecond before I was born that all was dark, and then suddenly all light. And no going back.

That's the important part: that *there's no going back.* No saying, "Uh uh, folks, I changed my mind. I took a good look around and I wish to return to the womb."

So. *Ergo.* The microsecond before God said, "Let there be Light!" did He stop and have a second, a considering thought? If He were Female He would have. She would have said, "Do I really want to do this? I'm getting along just fine without people, and once I make that decision, there they are—moving in, taking over, going their own ways. That's part of the package I just designed—was I *drunk?*" (God asks Him/Herself).

Too late!

The plans have been set in motion! There's THE LIGHT and all that comes after it. Did God ever have second thoughts? Would God buy a used boat from that man? What would Jesus do if He ("Uh-oh, hey, Dad, You promised me I couldn't sink!") found out all too late that He wasn't able to walk on water? Would Peter throw up his hands and go home?

Anyway. There is a microsecond before I receive the results of my pathology report (on top of that small heart attack—did your mother ever tell you that happened to me? I was sorry she had to see that. Well, I worried about *that* one and here came this cancer report out of nowhere, like a wrecking ball whamming into me before I even had time, out of the corner of my eye, to see it coming.) In that beautiful glorious expectant microsecond just before a report like that, all is innocence, all is future, all is possibilities.

So I muse now, my thinking speeded up the way things can happen so fast in an emergency—did part of me recognize that this boat dealer was a shyster? Abraham Gottfried Ranger. Why on hell's earth would I ever trust anyone with that crazy made-up-sounding name?

 Did I realize, kicking the proverbial tires, that the boat he sold me was held together with chewing gum and toothpicks? After all, this is the way I would have picked to leave this life if given a choice.

I don't mind drowning. I've never done it and we should all try new things every now and again.

But if the Coast Guard shows up and rescues me I am suing Abraham's sorry ass for all he's got.

Five.

Maya   6:45 am May 17, 2019
Banana Bay

<u>Dreams</u>   a poem by Maya Porter, 2005

God gives us dreams to remind us

Of what we sense, reason laid aside as we sleep:

That our pre-beginning and post-ending

Are more wondrous than anything here. The birds know.

They sing in constant joy, messengers in a universal language

Teasing us to remember our lives

Before birth, heralding us to anticipate

Heaven!

*   *   *

The smell of coffee rouses me. Voices, one low, one high, are murmuring somewhere close by. I open my eyes and groan.

Apparently I fell asleep in Franklin's chair in the living room, my glasses still on my nose. I look over at the Sofa. It appears to have been studying me, weighing my worth, while I slept. Bastard.

"—but Deano's Mom says I could have one of the puppies--!"

"Sh-h-h. You'll wake Maya."

"But, *Mom*--!"

"You know your grandmother doesn't want a dog here."

"Then why can't we *move*? We could live someplace else and then I could have a dog."

"We can't move. Not yet. I can't afford—"

"Then ask my Dad!"

"Frankie, I don't know where he is."

"You don't know that and you don't know where Grandpa is, either! *Why can't you just keep track of people?*" Frankie's voice is just this side of sobbing.

"Frankie, come here." I can't hear his voice now. Frances is probably holding onto him. It's true that she can't afford to live anywhere else. The job she has as a substitute teacher is part-time right now, with only a promise of more hours "soon".

She's up early. She must have gone jogging. I worry about her doing that in the dark. I knew a guy who did that and he got attacked by a pit bull that came out of nowhere and what was worse was that he was a veterinarian and —

"Frankie, go see if Maya's awake yet."

There's a sound of clumping feet and I just have time to remove my glasses before Frankie is standing in front of me. "She's in the living room," he announces. "Maya, Deano's dog had puppies! And they're the cutest--!"

"Not right now, Frankie," says Frances, entering the room. I was right—she's wearing her jogging outfit. She looks so healthy! "Want some coffee? I just made it. And what were you doing, not in bed? Bad dream again?"

"I—was trying to get used to this Sofa and I guess I fell asleep here."

"So, Maya—Maya, Maya, listen! Deano's mom says when the puppies are a little older--!"

"Frankie, I'm sorry. Not right now, okay? Not before coffee," I laugh, averting my unbrushed breath from his as he tries to climb into my lap. "Don't you have to get ready for school? Did you get your report about the raptors written?"

"Yeah. It's due today. Whoa! I forgot! Mom, can you copy me a couple of pictures?"

"You eat and I'll do that for you, Frankie."

"Frank the Tank!" I call after them, using the nickname his friends call him, in an attempt to placate him.

Frankie perches on a stool at the kitchen counter while I, now dressed and made up in my new aquamarine-colored dress and matching jewelry, bought to celebrate in with Franklin when he returns, prepare my breakfast. I wear an apron. The way Frankie jostles around, I need some protection.

"My report's gonna be the best one, because it's different. All the other kids are doing reports on the Moon landing, because the fiftieth anniversary of it is coming in July." He studies me. "Were you there, at the Cape, when the rocket went off?"

I laugh. "I'm not that old, Frankie. I --wasn't even born then, I don't think."

"So, you're not even fifty years old," he says, starting to do the math in his head. "But if Mom is—"

"Let me hear your report," I say quickly. "And watch the butter. Don't get your paper dirty."

"Okay."

Frances has given her son a handsome blue binder. "RAPTORS ARE OUR FRIENDS" Frankie has spelled out on its cover. "Maya, wouldn't that be funny if I spelled the word wrong and it said 'Raptors are our Fiends'?" He laughs. I join in obediently.

59

He opens the folder, smooths the pages and reads: "There is a group of birds called raptors. They are birds of prey. They feed mostly on the meat of other birds and animals. There are owls in this group, as well as falcons. Owls have soft feathers because they hunt at night and need to be quiet. Falcons are built for speed and the per--peregrine falcon is the fastest mammal in the world. It has been clocked at more than two hundred miles an hour when diving on its prey."

He looks up. "Maya—what's a mammal again?"

"It's a warm-blooded animal. A snake is a cold-blooded one."

"Oh. Okay. So *we're* mammals, too." I nod. He reads: "There is a bird sanctuary near here, where they take care of sick and injured birds. Miss Betsy is the lady there and she told a story about why we need raptors, because some houses were being built and the builders knocked down all the trees, so the owls had no place to live. Then when the houses were built, thousands of mice came and moved into the new houses. So the people were mad at the builders. So the builders went to the bird sanctuary to ask what to do, and Miss Betsy said to put up some posts and plant some trees for the owls to live in, so they did, and the owls came back to live, and in only THREE WEEKS all the mice were gone."

He looks up again. "That's great, right, Maya? Owls sure eat a lot of mice! And they have such soft feathers! I even petted one!"

I nod. My breakfast of scrambled eggs isn't looking too appetizing right now. But I asked him to read, so--.

"The word 'per-e-grine' means 'wanderer', and the peregrine falcon can be found in almost all parts of the world, even in big cities, where they perch on tall buildings and swoop down on pigeons. They were almost extinct, which means that they were dying out because of the D.D.T. spray that was put on fields that was poisoning them, but when the spray was made illegal to use, the peregrine falcon began coming back again."

He pauses. "So raptors are our friends and if you see someone shooting with a bb gun at an owl or a falcon, you need to tell them to quit doing that."

He stops reading and closes his folder. "And then I'll show them these pictures of raptors."

I'm touched. He's really done a lot of computer research and thinking about his subject. I remember back to my third grade class—we were barely reading back then and we had to share books, since there weren't enough to go around. Being asked to come to the blackboard was both terrifying and an honor. If I made a mistake, the whole class jeered. I remember—.

"Teeth brushed, Frankie?" Frances enters, dressed in such a lovely outfit, the color similar to mine that for an instant I look at her and think fondly, "We could be twins!"

"Frankie. I'm teaching at your school today, so we can go together. And turn off that tv. I can hear it all the way out here."

"Okay." Frankie grabs up his folder and runs to the bathroom.

"Subbing? What grade today?" I ask.

"Kindergarten. It's more babysitting, but they do take naps, so there's some quiet time. Shirley gave me a bunch of papers from her class to correct, so I need to go back to school this afternoon for a while. Are you off to *your* class?"

I teach a subject I've named "No More Poor Me". Franklin sent me to Orlando, to a week end course on self-esteem a few years ago when I was weepy and privately at odds with our marriage and myself; and I enjoyed the course so much that I decided to ask our priest if I could teach it. As a result I have my own classroom at St. Swithins' Episcopal Church and usually have a half dozen housewives to teach assertive techniques to, once a week. And this time I also have a man as a student.

I gave it up for a while after Franklin's boat—after Franklin was missing in the Atlantic—but Father George convinced me that I needed to keep busy until my husband came home.

I liked that he said "until", not "if", so I pulled myself together and probably did myself more good than I did the various women who showed up for my first class. I tell myself that it's more than just a social gathering and maybe they do get some good out of it—I know I have so much useful information to share with them!

"Mom!" yells Frankie, startling me. "Grandpa's on tv!"

"*They've found him!*" is my first heart-lurching thought. "Turn it up, Frankie! Turn it up!"

"But you just told me to turn it off!"

We stand around the tv set in Frankie's room. A slim young woman in a yellow dress too tight to wear in public stands before a desk in an Orlando studio and reads breathlessly from a teleprompter "—one-year anniversary of Banana Bay entrepreneur Franklin Porter, Jr.'s disappearance and probable death after his boat caught fire in the Atlantic, a few miles offshore. Some people on Banana Bay Beach around midnight said that they saw a kind of glow in the distance and thought they heard the sound of an explosion, but they figured it was some testing being done for the Cape. We'll have a live-person interview later in our program--."

The three of us stare. On the screen is a photo of Franklin receiving an award for something, and his class photo from his Harvard yearbook. "He was really good-looking," breathes Frances. I don't correct the past tense she has been using all year, although it unsettles me every time she does it.

She studies the anchorperson. "Oh! That's the same woman who came to our house last week. She had a man with a camera, too. They were looking to interview you, Maya."

"Really? Where was I?" I'm a little flattered at the possibility of an interview.

"Oh—I sent them away. I said we had nothing new to say. You were getting your hair done or something."

"Oh—that might have been—"

"Maya. They wanted to talk with you about how you and Dad met at a fundraiser in Philadelphia and how did that mesh with your upbringing in West Virginia?—which you *never* told me about until *I had to hear it on tv--!*"

There is an edge to her voice. She's been trying to get family information out of me for a year now, since she heard that tape recording that Franklin made. It broke my heart to hear his voice! I guess I *should* have talked about West Virginia with her when she was younger; but then should I have also told her about Red? Funny how the loss of face in a person just sits in there and stays fresh. It really should start fading after all this time, like fruit that has gone bad.

"So they found him!" says Frankie hopefully. "She said live person!"

"She just means they're going to interview someone who knew your grandpa." Frances looks sorry to have to tell him this.

I snort. "How can they possibly call this an anniversary? That's something you celebrate, not mourn."

"You're right, Maya. Want me to call the tv station and complain?"

"No, leave it alone. They'd probably just garble it worse. Turn it off. Look, Frankie—all three of us are getting ready for school!" I try to make my voice bright. There is a bitter place in my stomach as for maybe the thousandth time I picture poor Franklin all alone in that boat, using his old black tape recorder as a confessional. "Your teacher is going to love your bird stories."

I don't know whether to be relieved or annoyed that there are no family photos being shown of us. I remember a year ago how glad I was—I was probably in shock then-- that I had had my hair refreshed that morning, at that time in all innocence of what was to descend on us that night. Oh! I remember--it was because I was looking forward to having Franklin back. I was going to use my newly-coiffed hair as the excuse not to go out on his boat with him, although Frankie kept hopping up and down in anticipation of his return and finally fell asleep on our old sofa, not even waking when the inevitable phone call broke through early the next morning and shattered all our lives.

"Good luck with your report, Frankie," I lean down to kiss my grandson on the cheek as he turns away—he used to love my doing that, but I guess he's growing up. Or else he's mad at me about a dog. We had dogs when I was his age—mean, snarling, ill-bred hunting dogs that snapped at me. Why would Frankie want a dog?

Frances kisses me on the cheek and I turn, too, automatically. She cocks her head at me, birdlike. "You all right, Maya?"

"Stiff neck from the chair. I'll be okay." Frances nods and they are gone.

The house is now suddenly so silent that I'm sure if I tried, I could hear the Sofa breathing. I make myself a cup of tea and take it into the living room. I sit in Franklin's chair and I address the Sofa:

"I have a confession to make, Sofa: I'm forgetting what my husband used to look like. Remember the movie about going back to the future and Michael J. Fox is holding his family's photo and they keep fading out and disappearing? No, of course you don't. But that's what it's like to *me*, Sofa. The longer Franklin is away, the less able I am to recall what he looked like or sounded like, even though I try, and even though this house should be over*flowing* with echoes of him. And—oh, this hurts to say!-- if he's truly gone and I have spent this entire year waiting for him, then—who am I? Where's *my* life? See, this is what scares me, Sofa."

I yearn for, yet expect no response. I get none. Worse, I have just made myself weaker by confiding in Something that doesn't give a crap about me.

Six.

Maya   8:45 am   Banana Bay

<u>Not Alone</u>   a poem by Maya Porter

Two red cardinals

Brilliant

In deep green pine

Against glinting snow—

Sufficient proof that God,

Loving,

Meddles.

        *   *   *

The look of the Sofa doesn't fit our house and I'll tell you why:
our house is 1960s style. Parts of this style are back in now,
except for the popcorn ceilings from back then. Our house has an
air of old Florida ("St. Augustine Spaniard meets the Kissimmee
Cracker," Franklin would pronounce proudly, showing his guests

around) without, I think, the charm—like, I would have enjoyed a wraparound porch, only Franklin said, "What the hell do you know of charm?" and he's right as I wince at the memory of that old Chevy front seat in our living room back in Jerome.

Anyway: our house sits at the end of a cul-de-sac in Banana Bay, in biking distance to Frankie's school. These rounded streets with only one way out were quite popular back in the sixties, because they allowed for a big back yard. The drawback was not much parking for visitors. That was always a problem, because Franklin loved--loves to entertain. Fortunately for him the other two houses on either side of us are now owned by snowbirds, so we have the street to ourselves the greater part of the year, as we do now, in May. The empty circle also made it easier for Frankie to learn to ride his bike, around and around out of traffic.

Our neighbors sent flowers to our house, since they were already up north last year when Franklin—.

He wouldn't even let us take some of the property at Flamingo Roost and have a house built there. That's a community of mansions he'd gotten some really rich people to invest in. It's in the middle of the Indian River and there's an iron gate right off the main road of U.S. #1, so that sometimes the traffic backs up for a bit before the gatekeeper lets you in. The houses are so huge, like mansions! Their windows gleam reddish-gold when the reflection of the setting sun hits them.

Franklin liked telling me in private that all those places were built on dredged-up silt from the bottom of the river and they were all going to crack and slide into the water someday. That stopped me from wanting to live there, since I don't swim.

We bought our home when Franklin said he had so much extra money, and would have had more—there was a business deal he was working on where Disney Corporation would buy up a bunch of land on the Atlantic Ocean for a Disney-type resort on our beachfront, right across the causeway from Banana Bay.

Franklin was so excited about it! He set about buying up properties on the beach that he was going to then sell to Disney for an enormous profit and he had already made quite a lot of money, according to him, until one greedy realtor friend of his "spilled the Boston baked beans", as Franklin told me, and the Disney people, startled and wary as their famous deer in the headlights, withdrew their offer and went down to build in Vero Beach instead.

Fortunately, Franklin had just sold his beachfront land to someone else and we were safe, although the man he sold to never spoke to us again. At first Franklin thought we ought to build us a house *there*, but I said no sir, when the Rapture came I didn't want to be near that ocean. Water over my head? No, thank you!

He quit bullying me about it when the condominium craze out of Miami caught on here and he got a better offer to sell it. That was a relief. The pool in our back yard scares me enough. Snakes and gators could crawl into it at night!

Frances was in high school when we moved into this cul-de-sac house. She was driving by then and was so proud of her 1992 BMW, bright red. She took it with her to college (that was good—I got to park my car in the garage again), and she had it with her until she let a guy she met there drive it and he ran it into a tree. Nobody got hurt, but the car was done for.

I have to admit I was jealous when Franklin got her that car, and a little righteously pleased when he got mad at her about the accident. It was the first and only time I ever saw him angry with Frances. I myself had sure enough practice fending off an angry Momma when I was younger. Frances never got that kind of treatment from me. I knew how it felt.

Then they went off to Orlando together while I was getting my nails done and came back with a brand-new car for her.

Anyway, our house: the oversized two-car garage is off to the right. Franklin's Mercedes is parked inside there, ready for him when he returns, and I don't let Frances in it, either. Our mechanic said I should drive it to the store once a week to keep the tires even; so I do that, but never to the store to get groceries that might spill and *never* to let Frankie sit in it, even with clean hands.

There are Podocarpus bushes on each side of the garage door. Franklin has Manuel come and keep them trimmed. There are lots of bushes and plants out front, too—crotons and a magnolia tree, which Franklin barely tolerates when it drops its seed pods a couple of times a year. I still miss the northern elms and the chestnuts, but they don't seem to grow down here. . . .

If you look at the front of our gray color-painted house with the white tile roof, it has the big wooden front door with a little entryway kind of portico. (We don't use it much; we come and go through the garage. We've had almost no company in the past year.) Walk inside from the front door and there's an oversized coat closet to your right, bigger than my bedroom back in Jerome--who wears coats in Florida, anyway?-- and the living room to your left, down a couple of steps, so that's known as "sunken". The floor is all white tile squares with some imported rugs (Franklin says to call them "carpets, and they're from Afghanistan") on the floor. There's a grand piano that nobody knows how to play, although Franklin had hopes for Frances. Frankie and his friend Dean play some kind of simple pounded-out tunes and maybe that's enough for the poor neglected thing.

Then there's the Sofa and Franklin's leather chair and a large coffee table with some (I guess) expensive knickknacks that Franklin found in his countless travels, across from It, and some more chairs that Franklin says are "occasional" and a drop-leaf desk I use to pay my bills from the allowance I am given—this past year by Frances, who does the accounting for us--, and a bookcase of books that I mean to read someday. Franklin says some are first editions and doesn't allow Frankie or me to touch them, so I keep my Thesaurus in my desk.

There's a low table in front of the living room window with a phone and a couple of magazines on it. The phone here doesn't get used much, because we use the one in the family room, where Frances and I prefer to gather.

Off to the left from there is our master bedroom, in, as I said, the same battleship gray as the house is painted. It's a *huge* room with a *huge* bathroom. There's even a window that looks out to the street from the oversized shower, too high up for anyone to see me when I wash up, although I always hunker down a little anyways. Franklin showers as though he's on display.

I always meant to go out to the street when he washed up, to see if I could find out if his head showed in that window. He's almost six inches taller than me, so then I'd know I was safe standing all the way up, if I couldn't see *his* head.

I regret now that I didn't do that and now it's too—no, I can still do that when Franklin comes back. I should make a list of things to do when Franklin comes back. I'll bet I'll be able to start writing poems again!

"Window, window on the street/ Frame it low to see my feet." Hm-m. No.

There are French doors off the master bedroom where you step down to the back patio. They used to be sliding glass doors, but they always seized up off their tracks and got kind of rusty in the Florida humidity and Franklin was glad to replace them. I like these French doors and I'm glad the French invented them. When I pour my nightly vodka martini I have to be careful not to trip or spill, going outside to sit. My hairdresser Mr. Julian said that alcohol puts lines in your face, so I check mine every day. So far, so good.

I told him I was born the same year as Julia Roberts and Nicole Kidman (1967, I whispered, so nobody else could hear) and he said to me, "Maya, my dahling, you look so much better than either of those girls. But they don't have *me* to work on them, so there." I don't tell him I was born the same year as Vin Diesel. I don't need *those* kinds of jokes.

The furniture out on the patio is nice and comfortable and at night when the light in the pool is on, it's magical. Franklin had the pool designed for him as a kind of modified lap pool—that's what he calls it—and he loves to swim for what seems to me to be hours. I only go into the small shallow end. I like that part because it's kind of like a beach and slopes into the deeper water. Franklin had it designed that way.

With the lights on I can see if any snakes are swimming around in there. There haven't been any yet, but in Florida you can't be too careful. Frankie loves to fish stuff out of the water, so I always call him if there are any bugs disguising themselves like leaves, that kind of thing. He laughs at me, but I know better. I read about a woman who once found an alligator in her pool, and I've watched those tv shows where people are wrestling these *enormous* pythons, down there in the Everglades, the ones that escaped from a store or something after Hurricane Andrew and are now eating all our cute little Florida Keys deer, and if they're big enough to do that, then I don't want them on our patio!

But go back to the living room. Behind the living room (Franklin says I must not call it a great room), but not closed off from it is an oversized dining area with an enormous glass-topped table and ten really delicate chairs, all in white. There's also a big glassed breakfront (I think that's a funny name, like the front of it is going to break!) full of imported china, which Franklin says belonged to his mother and which Franklin says he stole from his house one time during his college days, after his mother died and when his father was out of town, just for fun and to see if he could get away with it.

"Did your father ever come after you and make you give them back?" I ask, surprised at this streak of criminality.

"Why should he? She'd left them to me," he says mildly. He rarely talks about her and when he does, she sounds like she was a lot of fun.

We only use her dishes at special times. Franklin says the pieces are irreplaceable, so he surprises me by washing them all by himself after the guests have gone home, instead of having the hired-for-the-evening maid or even me do them. I think that's funny, because he won't even help me make our bed.

If you go to the right of the dining area you will be in the kitchen. Look at how high the cabinets go up—you need a stepladder to get to the top of them. Franklin had this kitchen remodeled and it's all stainless steel gray and porcelain and marble. If you took all the shelves out of the refrigerator you could fit in it without a problem. The freezer is that size, too. I only cook simple stuff on the stove called something like-- A Fox? No. A Wolf. I hardly understand it. We had a cook once, but when Frances and Frankie came to stay, she quit before Franklin could let her go. Frances loves to cook.

There's a big high counter called a bar and there are stools on one side of it, so you can sit and look out the great big windows over the sink to the screened-in pool.

I'm not mentioning closets, but there are lots of them. Builders in that decade were fond of big closets.

Oh! I forgot! There's a white coquina fireplace in the living room. We've never used it. When Franklin brought a couple of logs into the house and placed them in the fireplace for show—they were white birch, he said, although I already knew that,-- I waited until he left and then I checked those logs *very carefully* for spiders. I kept a can of bug spray in one hand and I was ready to call Manuel if any spiders popped out at me. None did.

Then from the kitchen, you turn toward the back of the house where the gray carpeted area of the house begins and you are in the family room. Frankie has taken over this room and it is scattered with his games and electronic devices. I don't know how to operate most of them. I've asked him to show me, but he's always too busy with homework and other things.

Then there are three more large bedrooms down the hallway, one for Frances, one for Frankie, and the other as a den with a locked door for Franklin. Frances knows where the key is—another little bone of contention, because what if there was an emergency and Frances and Franklin were not at home and I needed to get in there?

Then Frances' bathroom, then *another* bathroom, also huge and tiled, which leads outside to the pool area. The tiles are *very* slippery when they're wet. I only fell the once before I learned that.

There are a whole lot of plants on the patio. I don't get to take care of them. Franklin has Manuel who only speaks Spanish come and care for them. At one point I thought I would ask Manuel to teach me some Spanish, or maybe I would get some books from the library, but then I got distracted by other things.

Also at one point I thought Manuel's name was "Pero", because when Franklin would tell him how to tend to the plants, Manuel would shake his head and say, "Pero, pero, pero!"

I finally asked Frankie to look up the derivation of the name on his computer.

"What name?" he said, blinking up at me from a game he was concentrating on.

"Manuel's other name. Pero."

Frankie burst into laughter. "That's not his *name*, Maya!" (I had forgotten he has some Hispanic friends.) "That means 'but'. I heard 'em. When Grandpa tells Manuel how to water the plants, Manuel argues with him. 'Pero'—that's so funny!"

I heard him call Dean a "Pero-head" a couple of times afterward and the two boys roared, rolling on the floor helpless in their shared joke.

I try to picture my Momma in my house. Maybe I should have contacted her just the once more before she passed not even months after Papa died—but the time just kept slipping away. My last letter to her came back with "NO FORWARDING ADDRESS" stamped on it. That's how I knew.

It's not that I would have been embarrassed about her, I don't think.

It's just that—I never could make up my mind if Franklin would like his friends here in Banana Bay meeting her or not. I never even got around to asking him if he'd mind.

Momma and I wrote to each other a couple of times a year, with me almost weeping over the number of words she didn't know how to spell right, and once sending me a newspaper article about how Red had died in Iraq. She passed away before Frances and Frankie moved in with us, otherwise I would have had to grab up the mail every day to keep Frances from seeing a West Virginia address and asking me all kinds of embarrassing questions.

Too late now, thanks to Franklin's recording. "What's my background, Maya? What's my background?" she pestered me all this last year.

"You're Scotch and English. Let it be." I will never let her know about all the Irish blood in her. I'll take it to my grave.

I went up to Jerome just the once, after Red died, for his service. I felt honor-bound, and Franklin was out of the country again for the government, he told me, for a couple of weeks, so I didn't have to explain myself. I hired Frances' favorite house sitter and I flew into Charleston alone, even though I don't like flying without Franklin. At least we weren't flying over water.

In Charleston I rented a car. First I visited my Papa, who by now had something I found out is called early onset dementia. I found him in a state-run institute in the city. He didn't recognize me at all. That was fair. I hardly recognized him.

Then I drove all the way into Jerome early the next morning for the funeral. At our old house my Momma greeted me with an odd kind of shyness, as though I was a visiting royalty person. I had packed simple clothes, but I was still the best-dressed one in Red's Catholic Church and my Momma (who didn't let on that she was full of cancer from her breasts, and would pass away soon after my visit) was so proud introducing me to folks, that she afterward sent me an area newspaper clipping that mentioned mine and Franklin's names as "former residents, now the movers and shakers of Banana Bay, Florida. Mrs. Franklin Porter is the daughter of Mr. and Mrs. LeRoy McDowell, lifelong residents of Jerome." Not that Franklin had ever been a resident there. And it was like me as Mayetta Jane never had been.

Momma was so alarmed, reading that word "shakers"! She thought I'd rejected her Methodist faith.

I didn't get a chance to correct her. By the time I wrote again she had passed and that was when Frances was having her tonsils operated on and Franklin was out of the country again, so I never did even find out when the funerals were.

I still feel bad about that, which is why I'm feeling obligated to jotting down all these notes about our house: Frances thinks I should sell it and move into something smaller, now that Franklin's—this is where I stopper up my ears to her—but she just got mad at me when I told her once again that he's still coming back, and she yelled, "Frankie and I still have lives, even if you've put yours on hold! I am *still* young enough to have another child or two!"

This shocked me so! Frances is always so even-tempered. I guess we have dealt with this past year our own individual ways.

Oh, how I wish I could write my poems again! "My mother's hands are old, so old/ They should be nice and warm, not cold/ Something, something--." Hm-m. No.

Trouble is I keep wanting to make them rhyme. "Box in words/ Box in birds/ Keep them tied to rhyming/ But see them pressed/To leave their nest/Of formal tidy—" Chiming? Climbing?" Oh, I have let my passion for writing dissipate so this year. I feel like I've been trying to write for a greeting card company.

As I leave the house through the garage and lean down for the newspaper, I happen to look up into the sky and there it is!—a large hawk-like bird slowly circling in the blue almost overhead. It's not indolent enough to be a turkey buzzard. No, this bird has a target in mind. There's a piece of unused property on the next block that's gone dormant into a kind of field. Some of the older kids have beat down some of the weeds and made a sort of ball field out of it, although there's a perfectly good one at the junior high school not three blocks from the field.

The hawk is still up there. Might it be a peregrine? I want to think so. My eyes dry out from watching it so intently and my neck cricks, so I lower my head for a couple of seconds to blink. When I look up again the hawk is gone. Miss Betsy was correct—they really move fast.

What would *I* do if I were that peregrine on her arm, bereft of crucial feathers, yet yearning with all my heart to fly and dive? That wondrous bird!—those oversized eyes looked at me as though they could see into my soul, the timid part of my soul that shrinks from action. *"I know you,"* those eyes seemed to be urging me. *"Do it. Do it. Do it."*

Unlike that damned Sofa, which says, "You don't even deserve to be taken seriously. You'll never leave West Virginia behind, you fraud. I know you."

"So do I," says the peregrine. *"You are strong like me. You've just never dared. All I need and all you need, is to be let off the shackles just one time—then watch us soar! Watch us slice the very air apart with our wings! Watch us--!"*

I have been unfolding the newspaper as I have been musing. Its headline brings me back to ugly reality: "WHERE IS FRANKLIN PORTER?"

The article announces that it is one year ago today that Franklin disappeared, presumed drowned at sea when his boat exploded and sank into the Atlantic Ocean off the Banana Bay coast. There is an old photo of the two of us, me in a shimmering blue formal dress and he in a tuxedo, looking very much like, and the caption emphasizes: "BANANA BAY'S TWO BEAUTIFUL PEOPLE—THE MILLENIUM COUPLE OF THE YEAR 2000". And there we are, nineteen years younger, looking so happy, so polished and successful, as though we have just been proclaimed the winners of a beauty contest. Which I guess we have.

We glittered when we walked.

Oh, will you look at this: "Franklin Porter, Jr. was a modest man who shunned the spotlight. His family remains prominent in Boston circles. Mr. Porter left behind his father Franklin Porter, Senior, his wife Maya Porter, his daughter Frances Porter and his grandson Franklin Porter II . Residents of Banana Bay are planning to hold a one-year anniversary candlelight vigil tonight at the Banana Bay Beach boardwalk on the Atlantic. No family memorial service has yet been scheduled, according to Father George Dudley at St. Swithins' Episcopal Church."

Well, that's just not right, the public taking a private citizen's— uh-- privacy away.

And I—I alone have been the guardian of Franklin's secret work for the government, as he asked me. I alone was told by him that he has a secret identity with them, that he is in no danger while undercover, that they are taking good care of him, that at any time he has layers of Marines watching out for him. He shared this with me privately after the Peggy fiasco and I have kept it, hugged it to my breast this past year, not even daring to share this knowledge with Frances, for fear of endangering Franklin unwittingly.

Oh, what are the townspeople expecting, that Franklin will abruptly emerge from the ocean like a Poseidon from the sea? Oh, I will be glad when this day is over. I hope everyone in my class has the decency not to mention this to me.

I study the photo for clues, hoping to find some hint of where Franklin is today. I never told Frances, but I was possessed, in the days after the boat accident, to go to the beach every day and walk it for a half-mile north, then a half-mile south, every day looking for—what?—clues? What were the odds of that? And yet I *had* to, was desperate to, the way the falcon just searched the ground for its next quarry.

I believed, I was so crazed and so unwilling to believe that the government would look out for him, that I had to get to Franklin's body before the birds got to it. Not my beautiful Franklin! I guess that's when I decided he *had* to be alive. I couldn't let myself picture him washed ashore, sodden, unseeing, perhaps unseen, driven by the waves of high tide into the seagrapes clutching the dunes, where the tiny white ghost crabs would dance across his chest, unable to tickle enough to disturb him.

I shake myself. What a gruesome vision! But I knew that in the early settler days here in Banana Bay, in the days after a storm or a hurricane the inhabitants would go in boats from the mainland east across the Indian River to the sandspit not yet named Banana Bay Beach, and then to the east again over the half mile-wide sand finger of land running north and south along the sea, to where they would scavenge everything they could from a ship's wreck: barrels of flour, cloth, rum—anything that floated to shore. They said prayers over any drowned sailors that they discovered. Nothing in those sailors' pockets except personal belongings—a cross, a pocket watch no longer working or necessary to the unfortunate bearers—sailors were not known to be rich men carrying silver and gold in their pockets. Sometimes their boots could be saved. Sometimes the nails in their boots were already too rusty to use.

Oh--enough of this! I take the newspaper with me, to re-read it later and keep it away from Frances and Frankie as long as possible. I might even tuck the article, folded, into one of Franklin's books for him to have a laugh over when he returns. This seems like a good plan to me.

Seven.

Maya   9:30 am   May 17, 2019   St. Swithins' Episcopal Church

The Month of May in Banana Bay, Florida   a poem by Maya Porter, 2013

Listen. Have you heard the trees, their hair

So alive with birds? The chatter

Is that of frolicking children.

Poincianas obscene in saturated flaming brilliance,

Proud, pompous as favored rich old relatives

Glancing slyly to catch

Their eccentric effect on me. This manic explosion

Of sight and sound

Would be judged bad manners

Anywhere but here.

*   *   *

"Uh-oh-- I've fallen and I can't get up!" Yes. That's a good line. It's even from a tv commercial. That should make my class laugh, in our second session.

No one laughs. Instead, they look stricken. I have arranged myself gracefully in my new aqua-colored print dress on the floor of classroom A, on the green terrazzo floor, which feels chillier than I had thought it would be. The room carries the aroma of chalk and Sunday School children's sweat.

Six sets of legs surround me, the owners sitting on the undersized chairs. I note automatically that Amanda's legs in shorts are shaved, muscular and tan. Joyce (I think that's her name) and her mother's are hidden by wide-legged slacks. The woman whose name I cannot remember and who never talks wears a long plain skirt. The only male student, the man she calls in a whisper, "Mex," sits next to her. He is wearing jeans and has pulled his chair a little apart from the group, but still close enough that he can hold the woman's hand. He looks very uncomfortable in a kid's chair. Kathy, overweight and constantly eager to please, wears, of all things, magenta hip-hugging gym tights. A faint scent of moist sneakers and unwashed feet reaches my nose. I have no idea where Brenda is—probably out in the parish hall prowling for goodies.

No one in my "NO MORE POOR ME!" (I am so proud that I thought of that title myself) class moves to help me. Instead, the women shift confusedly in their metal and plastic seats. They are so quiet that I can hear the AC unit in the window humming.

"Maya?" ventures Kathy, "Are you role-playing? Is that what this is?"

The woman in the long skirt whispers to the man. She seems middle-aged, but her clothing gives her appearance that of an old lady. I'm mildly annoyed by her whispering, but I keep smiling hopefully from my uncomfortable place on the floor.

"Of course she's role-playing," Amanda says. "You don't hear her moaning"

Moaning—that's good! "Oh, I sure wish I could get up," I moan, not making eye contact with anyone.

"Maybe she really can't get up." Kathy moves to my back and puts her arms under my armpits. *Good—Kathy isn't that strong.* I make myself a dead weight in Kathy's grasp.

"Nah, nah, nah," says the man Mex, rising from his chair as Kathy steps aside. He grabs me under both arms and lifts me without any effort, surprising me. Goodness! I hadn't noticed how muscled he was until just now. "You okay now." He looks at me with concern.

"Thank you," I straighten my clothing. Mex goes back to his seat and the woman in the skirt whispers to him again as he shakes his head in response.

"Okay, now what did I just do?" No one responds. "See-- I didn't actually ask for help".

"Sure you did," says Kathy.

"No. If I had been assertive, I would have said something like, 'I've fallen down. Will someone come help me?' See, I would have made a *statement* first and *then* asked a question."

"So if there's a fire in my house, I should lean out the window and make a statement like, 'There's a fire in my house.' Then a question: 'Will someone kindly come and help me?' " Kathy looks pleased. The other women nod.

"Well, I'm not sure you need all those words in an *emergency* situation—."

"It looked like an emergency to me."

"What I was doing was acting like a Poor Me, like someone who can't take care of myself. Remember what a Poor Me is?"

"Oh! Sure! It's a person who says they can't help themselves and really they *could*, not like *real* people in fires or hurricanes—".

"Right," I say, wary. I know how fast this group goes off the subject.

"Hurricanes! Remember that one in—what, 2002, 2003-- hit Miami? Not Andrew. We all know that one." Kathy especially has a hard time staying on task.

"How about 2004? The one that hit us in 2004 was worse!"

"I had blue tarps on my roof for months!"

"What was the name of that one?"

"Harold, I think."

"Nope, that year it was a girl's name."

Now I know the name of the 2004 hurricane because it was the same name as my daughter, Frances—but we have veered way off track. I have, as I did last week, lost control of my class. The women are animated now, all talking over each other and finishing each other's sentences. The noise level rises.

I look across at Amanda, who never has a hair out of place, never seems to sweat, who would never plunk herself on the floor for her students, who looks coolly amused. She appears to be sharing some private joke with me. She looks like she knows all about my West Virginia upbringing and the fact that I am not *really* sure of myself in this room as an instructor. She looks like—lordy, she reminds me of the Sofa! What is she doing in my class, anyway?

Truthfully, I am more than a little scared of her.

"Excuse me, Miss Teacher." It is Mex. "My sister wants to know if this is a way to save her money."

89

"Uh—what?" So they are brother and sister.

"See, she not speak English so good. I been here in this country longer than her. I tell her about your class "Poor Me", you know, and she is thinking these are ways to save money here in Banana Bay—you know, shopping for food and cloths—things like that."

Well, that explains the constant whispering: he has been translating for her.

"Oh, I see. Well, this class is about working on our self-esteem and feeling better about ourselves, about standing up for ourselves!"

"Ah. *Not* food." He speaks to his sister once more and she suddenly hides her face in her hands. "This English, it is not an easy one to learn."

Amanda stands up. "Mr. Kartok, I think that what you just said was quite assertive. Thank you for letting us know about what is going on with your sister—."

"Elena. Her name Elena." The woman takes her hands from her face at the mention of her name.

"Elena. Good to know you." And now they are following Amanda's lead, up and out of their seats and shaking Elena's hand and she is smiling shyly and I have now *totally* lost my class and we are almost out of time and I am feeling negligent that I did not think to do all of this introducing the first morning we met, last week.

"Welcome, Elena and--Mex?"

"Max. Max Kartok. Glad to be here." Oh. Max, not Mex. I should have guessed. "If we could get back to my being on the floor--."

"I think you specifically asked for help." Amanda raises an eyebrow. "Specifically."

"Oh, no, I don't think I—"

"I thought she asked for help, too," adds Kathy. The two women in slacks nod.

"So, if Maya *asked* for help, then she would be assertive and she wouldn't be a Poor Me!" yells out one of the slacked women, possibly hard of hearing and apparently delighted to have unraveled a mystery. I feel sweat begin to trickle down my back.

"Okay, so if I was in the Atlantic Ocean and I was *drowning*—," begins the younger of the women in slacks—Joan? Jean? Joanne? Joyce?

"Jane! No!" cautions her partner in slacks, pushing at her arm and looking at me, her face flushing with embarrassment. The woman named Jane (*that's* the name, just like my old one—I'll have to remember that) stops in midsentence, as though appalled at her social breach.

"Oh! Maya! Sorry, Mom." Ah. So they *are* mother and daughter. It makes more sense now—I suspect that Jane finds her mother places to go, and this class is handy. Possibly Father George even moved them in my direction to get them out of his office.

 The gaffe is that they remember Franklin's boat accident. They probably have already scanned this morning's newspaper.

"That's all right," I say. Inside I feel my heart crush against my ribs. I sit down, my legs feel suddenly so weak.

Jane's mom continues relentlessly on as though plodding her way through the sand at the beach, "I *told* you I had a good memory. One year ago today it was."

I'm afraid I am going to cry in front of my class, but all of a sudden Amanda rescues me by saying in a forceful voice, "All right, what if I just said, and I'll make my voice babyish and whiny, 'Oh, I can't get these two shopping carts apart,' and I waited for someone to help me, although I hadn't asked for any help—I'd be in Poor Me mode now, wouldn't I?"

"Oh, sure," says the group in unison, diverted. "*Now* I get it," says another.

"So you don't have to be on the *floor* to be a Poor Me," adds Kathy. "It's what you do with your voice," and the class nods in unison.

"So don't use a high voice, like a baby. But what if you only have a deep voice?" asks Jane.

"Yours isn't deep."

"No, but what if it was?"

"Ya get listened to with a deep voice," a woman says from behind me. We all turn. It's Brenda, Brenda with her long graying hair in a ponytail, wearing shorts and a washed-out tee shirt reading "SHAVE THE WAILS". She did not say a word the first week that I started teaching this class. She's not a member of St. Swithins' and she doesn't hang around afterward for small talk. I've watched her carefully wrap cookies in a paper napkin and hide them in her purse.

"You'll have a turn to talk," says Kathy primly.

"I'm gonna talk *now*. See, that kinda thing happened to me once—I worked in a nursin' home and this old lady fell down, just like you, Maya, except she had a walker. So I helped her up even though she didn't ask—I just got there before anybody else—and then she told everybody, in this baby-high voice, that I stole her wallet." An image of the people with dementia in my Papa's unit flashes across my mind.

"What happened?" The class is riveted.

"What the hell you think? They fired me." Brenda's face has gone from animated to emotionless in an instant.

"Did they ever find the--?" Jane asks.

"Sure. They found it that afternoon in her room, stuffed between her mattress and box spring, along with a buncha old food. The

93

nursin' home called and told me to come back to work, but no way in hell was I goin' back to that place again."

There is a silence.

"And that old lady, *she* had a baby voice and *she* was actin' like a Poor Me, so this stuff that Miss Maya is teachin' really is true."

I am touched by Brenda's endorsement of me. We all have dealt with unfairness in our lives, I think. It was certainly unfair of Franklin to go and buy that boat in South Carolina without even asking for my opinion. But there's no way I would share that, especially today, as an example of my being a Poor Me.

"Ya move on, right?" Brenda demands, her eyes challenging. "Like the Teach says, ya lower your voice and get up offa the floor. Good advice. Like I'da taken that old lady's money."

"*They come, they take money*!" It is a sudden outburst from Max's sister. "They take house, take all, take Mama, Papa! I here now wit' Mex!" In a strong voice she points a finger skyward and declares, "They no make me sit on floor *ever again*!" Max pats Elena's arm and we all spontaneously applaud.

There is a loud knock at the door. Elena starts, sudden alarm on her face. Her brother takes her hand and says something to her in a calm voice. Father George enters, smiling as always. He catches my eye and intones, "Sounds like a very successful class this morning, eh? Coffee's ready." He scans the faces. "No Fran here today?" He looks disappointed. He insists on calling my

94

daughter "Fran". I really need to correct him, but then he might become cool toward me. He might just find another use for my classroom and then where would I be?

"I brought cinnamon apple coffee cake!"

Kathy. Every week she brings a carb-loaded dessert. My students rise from their chairs.

"Class, wait!"

They regard me as one who has already been forgotten in their haste to get to the table in the parish hall. "We need to say our mantra, remember? The one I taught you last week?" Last week I had been determined that they would have some homework, but there was such a teenager-like cry of pushback that I had settled on a few words they would memorize. So now we recite:

"When life hands you lemons, make lemonade." I see Kathy's lips pucker at the thought of lemonade as a drink rather than a motto.

And I had taught them, "Most people are going through life centered on their own problems. They are really not noticing you, and certainly not you as a person. So if anyone insults you or ignores you or honks their horn at you, what do you say to yourself?"

Now they chant solemnly, "JUST DON'T TAKE IT PERSONALLY."

What a fraud I am. I *am* taking this morning's teaching personally. I feel a pang of resentment. I have so much more to teach! How has this all gotten away from me? The women are shaking my hand, hugging me (at least the sentimental Kathy is), thanking me for having learned so much today.

What have they learned?

Then I hear my Orlando week end instructor's voice in my head: "It's not the content so much as it is the process, Maya," and I didn't understand this at the time. So maybe just their bonding is what's needed.

But I don't *want* to bond with Amanda and I must, because she is standing at my side. "Thanks for helping me out," I say to her. She waves away my words. "You have a very well-mannered grandson there, Maya—Frank the Tank."

"Oh—thank you. How do you know him?"

"I'm Deano the Beano's aunt. Those are some adjectives they gave each other, huh? Like their own private club. The two boys play together at my house every now and then. Frances didn't tell you? I'm the one with three cats."

I can't recall that she told me anything about that. "Uh, I know about all the puppies—"

"Ugh. My sister. What was she *thinking,* bringing a pregnant dog home from the shelter?" She stares at me. "So, Maya, just where did you get your college degree in psychology--?"

96

"Excuse, please." It is Max. I look up to see which one of us he wants to talk to, glad that he has saved me from answering Amanda in a lie. Amanda smiles at him politely and moves off to chat with someone else.

"Miss Maya, I want to tell you how much it means to my sister Elena, to be able to sit in your classroom and watch you."

"Well—thank you, but—"

"I was the one who came here to this country first. She was supposed to come with me, but she had to go to hospital. It hurt here." He puts a huge weathered hand on his lower right side, below the waist.

"Appendix?"

"Yah. And by the time she was back home, hospital was bombed. My Papa got her out just in time. The rebels took over all our town."

"Oh—I'm so sorry."

"They next went after our homes. They took our Mama and our Papa, too. We never see them again. So for her to sit in your class and not worry that she will be taken away—she is grateful. I am, too."

A lump rises in my throat and my eyes fill with tears. I am at a loss for words. What a kind open face he has! He looks as though he would understand the deepest troubles in my heart. I am about

97

to confess to him, but Max saves me from blurting out my fears about Franklin's possible drowning (which I refuse to believe!) by asking, "You like wegetables?"

"Wedge-- well, yes."

"I grow wegetables. I bring you some."

"Well—okay. Thank you."

"Before they go bad. First they good. Then they bad." He grins at me. Now that I stand beside him, I can see that he is actually at least six feet tall, with broad shoulders. He's possibly my age, but I'm not about to tell him mine in return for my asking his.

"Come on, ladies—lots of goodies over here," calls Father George. His white Episcopal collar has a hint of lipstick on it. Since his drying out from an alcohol addiction and his subsequent divorce from Gail, the Penney's saleswoman who also sang week ends with a heavy metal group known as "The Gorillas", the general church population, female at least, has turned to "poor Father George's eligibility". After a lot of forgiving of him. For the drinking, not the unfortunate choice of a marriage partner.

But I have to admit he's very good-looking, almost as handsome as Franklin, and has those striking blue eyes! How old would he be now—forty-two, forty-three?

I watch Brenda wrapping cookies and pastry in a napkin. I suddenly feel tired. I've worked so hard on this set of teaching sessions and I'm not sure the class has learned anything from them yet. I gained so much insight at that week end seminar! Now all my notes are drying out and crinkling at the edges and I've had to pay Staples myself to have lessons copied, since the church's secretary takes a jaded view of anyone using the office copier for anything except St. Swithins' bulletins.

I accidentally catch Brenda's eye. She moves to me and taps me on the shoulder. "Now you listen," she says in her husky voice, "I know it's a year today. I read. I know. I remember."

I start to protest, but she keeps talking. "I hear things. Mosta the votes in town go for sharks, but don't you listen to 'em. Miracles happen all the time. You gotta have faith, right, Father?"

Father George has moved in smoothly. He takes my hand. "One year. I get it," he says sincerely. "Maybe—might I come visit you this evening?"

Brenda bursts out with a raucous laugh. "Excuse me there, Padre. Whew! You just showed what we all learned just now in Miss Maya's class: make a statement, then ask a question." She pops her lips together and apart several times and points a finger-pistol. "You're okay there, Padre." She turns and spots Max. "Hey! This Padre, he's okay!"

"Padre" is waiting for an answer. "Oh. Tonight would be fine. Thank you, Father George." Although he's almost a decade younger than me, I still respect his position. It would probably be good to have a man, any man, in our house tonight.

"Unless—you'd want to go to the vigil on the beach?"

"Oh! No. No, I—couldn't."

"Understood. Fran told me she'd bow to your wishes."

He nods toward Max. "He's got quite a story. He owned meat packing plants in Europe for years, worked alongside his men, hauling sides of beef over his shoulders. Looks like he could be a wrestler, doesn't he?" He winks at me—are priests supposed to do that?—and says, "I'll see you. And Fran? Ah. Yes. Good. At your house. Tonight."

He doesn't know I have a plan in mind for him. I want my priest to do an exorcism on the Sofa. Except not with holy water, which might leave stains on the linen, in case I want to take it back to the store.

Eight.

Maya 10:45 am   May 17, 2019   Banana Bay Elementary School

The Accuracy of Fortune Cookies   a poem by Maya Porter
2017

A traveling speaker at our Episcopal church

Warned us of the evils of this world:

Astrology in the daily newspaper and for some reason

 Masturbation

Which she grouped with Ouija boards and tarot cards.

I was glad she left out

Chinese fortune cookies, which represent

One of the last morsels of mystical choice.

My hand in the restaurant hovers over the plate of

Folded futures: "A fortune can be yours" or

"A trip is in store".

It's reassuring to know one's tomorrows await

Within a wrapped-up wedge of starch.

One who does not care for Chinese meals

Is bound for a life with no destination.

*   *   *

This is the time I would ordinarily be going to a movie in the Banana Bay mall.

I like the morning ones because there's almost no one there. The children are at school and there may be just a few older couples attending, so I get my choice of a seat.

I ought to move if someone sits directly in front of me—I have that freedom, although I feel as though I should apologize to the newcomer: "Nothing personal, sir, but I can't see." I never do move, of course—so many vacant seats and what if the person in front of me is a down-on-his-luck out-of-work man?—but I feel I *could*. I don't want to insult him though, if he has weighty issues on his mind and is escaping here for a few hours, as I am. It sounds silly, but I don't want him to take it personally. I know not to.

The movie theater smells of old fake popcorn butter and commercial air conditioning. Not musty exactly, but a trifle damp, as though many wet umbrellas and sugary spilled sodas have dripped onto its carpeting. I always get to my seat before the previews begin. Sometimes I'm too early and have to sit through the car and the dental commercials. There's one showing a mother and daughter presenting their toothy fake new smiles. Do Frances and I look like that? No way, I smile at myself in the dark, rather smug about this. *They* don't look like sisters, no way. Not like Frances and me.

This past year I've seen a lot of movies, two and sometimes three a week, depending on how fast they change them out. I started talking with the young man, Tim, who takes my money and gives me my ticket and my change. I even let other people in ahead of me in line so I can be the one at his station and chat with him about what I've seen or am about to view. He loves movies, too, so this is a small yet welcome treat for me.

Tim and I are both immersed in the Film Noir series on Wednesdays and we enjoy discussing whether Ida Lupino or Barbara Stanwyck makes the more convincing Dame Who Gets Slapped Around. They are both very self-confident looking women. We talk about the camera angles and shadowy alley shots—Tim doesn't realize it, but he's helped me get through this difficult past year. He's a decent young man and I'm very careful not to get him in trouble with his boss. I move right along when the line is long. Which, as I've said, is not often. I find I miss him when he has a day off.

On Wednesdays patrons such as me with a special card can get a small free popcorn and Tim caught on very fast as to how much butter I like on mine.

The incident last week convinced me that I'm not going to do that anymore—wait in Tim's line. I'm still mortified, reliving it: I was in my favorite stall in the empty ladies' room last week. It's the handicapped one with more space and its own sink. (I'm always careful about appropriating it when there are lots of women around, for fear of depriving a real handicapped person.) I could hear two young ticket-taking employees chatting in front of the big triple sinks.

"Tim is leaving."

"Oh yeah? Which one is he?"

"You know. Freckles, a little pudgy, glasses. Taking another job. He didn't tell *me*, but I know why. Wanna know why?"

"Sure."

"That old lady? The one that keeps talking to him? She was getting him all worried."

"You mean the one comes to the movies all the time in the daytime? By herself?"

"Yeah. You know the one I mean, don't you? She's the one, her husband got lost at sea last year."

"Oh! Her? *That's* the one? Shit. *Now* I remember. Yeah."

"Yeah. So I told him, 'Ya gotta watch out for the cougars, Tim.' That's what I told him."

"What's a cougar?"

"You kidding? It's a rich old lady just cruising around on the make for younger men."

There is a pause. I sit without breathing in my stall. I pull my feet up close to the toilet.

"Uh oh. Are we alone in here?" one whispers.

"What if it's the manager?" whispers the other. There is the thump of the outer door being pushed open and then no other sound. I sit. I flush. I adjust my clothing. I wash my hands carefully, gently. I dry my hands, taking my time. I don't dare look at my face in the mirror.

Tim is gone the next week. I don't ask where he went. I don't discuss movies with the teenager wearing the name "Rhonda" on her nametag, who takes my ticket money without a word, who looks at me sideways and who hands me my free bag of popcorn with not enough butter on it. I accept it without complaint.

105

I'm not at all good at nursing. I don't like blood, although I am a regular donor (I never watch when they put the needle in, never look at the bag in the shape of a small red football, which must be so warm from the blood which moved so recently through my body) and I have a "5 GALLON" sticker on my car window. I never liked it when Frances was sick and running a fever, or worse, when she was throwing up and had diarrhea at the same time. I always worried that I would get sick, too, and then who would take care of us, with Franklin gone so often on his business trips?

But Frankie pleaded with me, "You got to help, Maya. My teacher says they need volunteers in the cafeteria and the nurses' station and the playground. I get extra credit if I get somebody from my family to come help. Plee-ze, Maya."

So here I am. Fortunately it's only for two hours a week and the most I have ever had to do was to dispense a girl's asthma medication as directed, and to hold a cold washcloth on a boy's forehead when he got hit on the playground with a volleyball.

So I mostly tidy up the room and straighten the sheets on the narrow cot, and make sure the roster is in order and hope that no one really sick comes in.

I wanted to say hello to Frances in the kindergarten, but apparently the kids were listening to a story when I went by, so I didn't interrupt. I did look in and wave. She had a child on her lap and several other little ones were draped around her shoulders as she read. I'm not sure she even saw me.

I wish I'd brought a book. Maybe if I had paper and pencil I could think of a poem about this: "White bed, white room/ White——." Hm-m-.

Franklin would get angry when he saw me with a pencil. He bought me a couple of pens and I'm sure they were expensive, but I wrote my first poems with a pencil that I had sharpened myself with my pocket knife, and that's my preference to this day, like my thoughts: in erasable graphite rather than permanent ink.

I hear the bell ring for the first lunch. I don't understand how they can eat lunch so early, and I don't even know when Frankie has his meal time. He's always ravenous when he comes home, I've noticed.

And surprise-- there's Frankie at the door as I'm thinking about him. "Here's Maya—she'll take good care of you," he says as he brings a boy his size into the room. "Deano says he doesn't feel so good, so the teacher had me bring him in to you."

Dean Holcomb. Deano the Beano. He does look a little pale. "Does anything hurt, Deano?" I ask as I shake down a thermometer. "Did you have breakfast this morning?"

"M-m-m-f," he says. I take out the thermometer. Normal. That's good.

"I just want to go ho-ome," he wails. He holds his stomach. Oh, no. Is he going to throw up?

I wonder what I should do next. "Let's have you lie here for a few minutes and then see how you feel." I look around for a basin.

"He could go home!" states Frankie. "He just lives across the street from the school!"

Deano nods. "I just live across the street. And then my Mom could take care of me."

Well, this seems logical. At this moment with much clicking the loudspeaker calls out: "Mrs. Porter, can you stay a few minutes after 12:30 today? Your replacement is running late and just called."

"Yes, I can do that," I call back in a loud voice, hoping the loudspeaker lady can hear me. I've never been spoken to over the loudspeaker before.

A girl comes running in. "I'm bleeding! I'm bleeding! *I'm bleeding*!" she is screaming.

Deano gets up off the cot and I lay the girl down. She is hysterical for some reason. "I broke my nose! I broke my nose!" she cries. "This is my sister's blouse! She's gonna kill me!"

"What's your name, honey?" I ask as I wet a cloth for her nose. Deano moves toward the door, moaning. "I can take him home, Maya," says Frankie helpfully over the girl's screams. "That's Jessica. She's in my reading group."

"Wait, wait. You aren't supposed to leave school property, you two."

"So I'll just stand outside *on* school property and make sure Deano gets across the street okay. He needs to go home, Maya!"

"All right, just watch him. Watch for cars. Come back and tell me that he got across the street okay."

"Sure!" The boys run out of the room and I concentrate on Jessica's nose (not broken, just a bloody one) and her sister Nancy's blouse (polyester, will clean up just fine, I assure her). I write down that she accidentally walked into a door, her name, the time of day, her teacher, her classroom number.

Jessica is offended at my literary license. "I did *not* walk into a door. James shoved me right into it! On purpose!" Not knowing how much of this is true, I omit James' name from my report.

I am writing down the particulars of Jessica's accident and hearing for the third time in much detail how it happened when Frankie, out of breath, dashes into the room. "Okay!" he calls out, a man with a mission accomplished. "He got across the street okay!"

"Did you see him at his front door?" I ask.

"Yeah, he has his own house key and I saw him go inside. He was yelling for his mom. Maya, why can't *my* Mom call you Mom? And Grandmas let their grandkids call them Grandma. Why can't I--?"

"I'm busy here, Frankie. Shouldn't you go back to your classroom?"

"Oh. Yeah! Bye!" and he is gone.

I give Jessica a spare tee shirt—we keep them in all sizes, in case of emergencies like this—and I rinse the blood from her sister's blouse and roll it up in a plastic zippered bag for her. "Is Frankie your son?" she asks, taking the bag and shy now that the crisis is past. "He's my grandson," I answer, secretly delighted that she thinks I am young enough to be a mother and not a grandmother.

"He's Frank the Tank," she nods. "He read his report on birds *just* before James shoved me into the door." I smile to let her know I have memorized the door story. "Frank the Tank. I love him." She gives me an unexpected hug, pats my face, exclaims, "You're so pretty!" and runs back toward her classroom. Well. I'll have to ask Frankie at dinner why he didn't even acknowledge poor little Jessica.

I clean the room. My replacement, breathless, apologizing, arrives on time—traffic accident on I-95! All the southbound cars diverted! Had to take another road!

I even get to exchange greetings with Frances, who is on her way from the building. "Are you done for the day?" I ask.

"Yep."

"Me too. How about lunch?"

"I was just going to stay here and take care of some papers, but I can come back. Katz' Meow? Great. Deal."

Well. So far this day has shaped up just fine. And wait until I tell her that Father George is coming to the house tonight—I've observed how he looks at her in church, how he holds her hand longer than the other parishioners' when we say good-by after the service. Maybe his coming to see me at the house has more to do with her than with me. Huh.

I'm glad I've done nursing duty here at Frankie's school instead of going to a movie this morning. Today, of all days, I'm not sure I could have faced those young women at the ticket counter.

(There is no freshly hunted blood here in my metal prison. I yearn, I ache for the snap of the helpless neck, the shuddering of my shocked victim, the iron-odored blood that will be when I carry this bird now dead to its final stop on the brambled earth.

I was born for this. I have never made a pretense of being tameable.

111

Nine.

Maya   12:55 pm   The Katz' Meow Restaurant, Banana Bay Town Center

Some Atavistic Craziness   a poem by Maya Porter   2016

Some atavistic craziness seems to take over

When a man gets a power tool into his hands.

There he is in the back yard demolishing laurel trees

Panicking the grapefruit, threatening the pines.

And when he's inside he's perusing the catalogues

Coveting the riding mowers for his pocket-sized lawn.

This controlling compulsion for boundaries, territory,

When the vegetation gets along quite well by itself—

With the saw in his hand he can put off, deny

That his teenager son with a first-time mustache

Has the family car and is off "nowhere special"

And his daughter's looking secretive in amber-shaded lipstick

And his wife, tight-mouthed and frowning

Is making fortyish rumbling sounds.

*   *   *

I like this place for lunch. It's a former little bungalow, the kind that Sears- Roebuck and Montgomery Ward used to ship here in pieces in the 1920s. It's on a side street, away from traffic, converted into the kind of restaurant that sells reasonably-priced quiches, salads, sandwiches and assorted coffee drinks, nothing alcoholic.

Their bread pudding is the best in town. Nothing alcoholic, my foot—I swear there's plenty of Jim Beam in there. It's quite the most popular dessert with, as Sondheim says, "The Ladies Who Lunch". (That's how well Franklin has educated me over these years, so that I even understand how caustic Sondheim's lyrics can be around marriage and the emptiness of lives!)

 Hm-m. I need to write a poem about that sometime. "He writes of stairs, perfumed and strange/ Although he--". Hm-m. Range, grange, or-ange. Ah. *Arrange*--. Hm-m.) I could use a piece of paper and a pencil. I should carry them with me.

I always tell myself I won't need dinner after eating here for lunch. So far that hasn't been true, but it's a harmless bit of self-deception. There are laundered flowered tablecloths, always a fresh-cut flower in a tiny vase, and pretty napkins—maybe that's why men don't seem to frequent the place.

I happened to be here once when a foursome of retired men showed up. They all used their outside voices—they might have needed hearing aids-- and seemed very much out of place. I don't think they ever returned, apparently to the female customers' relief. Women prefer this place to be more a sanctuary than a gym.

Myra and Joe Katz run the place. She's quiet and efficient and he tries to be. He stays in the kitchen. They don't even like cats, I have found out. I want to write a poem about them, but haven't found the right approach yet. I picture my poem framed and hung on their wall, along with local art work, for people to read and admire. "Who has a name like a Siamese/ Please don't tease--."

Miss Pendleton, back when I was in high school years ago, sat down next to me one day and said, "Miss McDowell, *poems do not have to rhyme.*"

Oh! It was like God Himself was giving me permission to get away from "June/Moon/Tune/Croon"! I remembered that. That wonderful Miss Pendleton. What could have happened to her?

I've had a hard time making decisions and writing this year. I'll get back to poetry after Franklin comes home and remembers who I am, with his amnesia gone.

Frances and I have both ordered the vegetarian quiche and fruit salad, which reminds me: "A man in my class. His name is Max. He said he'd bring me some vegetables."

"That's nice," says Frances absently.

"And Father George said he'll stop by tonight, since it's—you know."

Frances seems to perk up at the mention of Father George's name.

"Maya, if you want—we'll stay home tonight together, away from the vigil."

"Do you want to go?"

"I'd rather keep you company. I already talked it over with George."

I am relieved. "How was your kindergarten class?"

"Oh, just a roomful of cute kids with the usual problems—a crayon up the nose, a wet pants situation, one boy not getting enough sleep at home, a scuffle. . . ."

She sits up and looks squarely at me. "Maya, we have to talk about Dad."

"Oh, do we have to right now? How was Frankie's report? This little girl--."

"Yes, we *have* to. Don't try to change the subject. Today is one year to the day that Dad went missing. As everyone in town seems to know."

"Yes. As your father's wife, I am well aware," I say formally. I sense where this conversation is going, and I don't want the two of us to discharge any negative   feelings toward each other that would be hard to walk back.

"Maya, the whole issue hinges on your signing the paper that says you believe Dad is dead."

"I just *don't* want to talk about this!"

"But my financial future and Frankie's depends on it!"

Franklin's will, on his desk in his locked den, which door in *my* house only Frances could unlock with *her* key!—stated that Franklin was about to purchase a boat and head back from South Carolina by himself and that if anything happened to him, if he was missing for a year and a day, he was to be presumed dead and his estate was to be divided, with Frances getting quite a chunk— enough, I feared, for her and Frankie to move out and away from me.

But Franklin had left a ringer in his "will"—that I as his widow had to acknowledge that he was dead. And Frances knew very well that I was not about to do that. I had even refused to have a memorial service for him.

Oh, I knew what that would mean. I had surprised myself by being so firm about it. The way *I* read his will, he still had this one day to be alive. By his will, he wouldn't be dead until tomorrow. And I was going to make sure his wishes were carried out.

"But it doesn't really mean that!" Frances had told me several times, almost wailing. I kept forgetting that she had her own grief to deal with, as well as Frankie's. Bad enough that her ex-husband Pete had dropped off the face of the earth. Now her father had, too. "Everyone knows he's gone except you!"

"We Porter women seem to lose men, don't we?" I ask, in an attempt to lighten our table talk mood. Frances does not smile. "Frances, don't you see that I *can't*? I can't agree that he is dead."

"You can't keep up with your amnesia theory, Maya. Frankie and I need our own place where we could have a dog for him. We'd live nearby," she pleads.

"Look, Frances—the reason he wrote it the way he did is because he truly believed that if anything happened to him he would survive. You know what a strong swimmer he is."

"*Was.* Was, was, was!" Frances suddenly slams her chair back and stands up. "You really need to face it, Maya!"

117

Several people stop talking and look around. This town is small enough that the chances are that they all have read in this morning's paper about Franklin and his boat. Franklin, you have put me in an impossible position: being true to myself or helping our child. What was behind your reasoning?

"And you refuse to talk to me about where you came from and your background and it's mine, too, Maya. *It's mine*, too! I just want to know who I am!"

Her face looks down at me. She is not smiling and—oh my!-- I get a hint of Red's face looking at me that summer afternoon. The resemblance is strong enough that I swear the odor of the West Virginia woods in summer passes through me. Oh my god, I think with a cold stab of fear, would Frances take me to *court* over this, my own daughter? She's angry enough to. She probably would win. That's the problem with me, being able to see both sides and all she has to see is her own. Damn it, Franklin! And I have to be honest; I don't know if I'm more scared that she would find out about Red or about my early shameful years of poverty.

"Wait, wait," I say quietly so I won't draw attention to our quarrel here in public—and on this day, too!-- but she has left without even finishing her lunch and I still have to stop and pay the bill. Well, we came in separate cars, so at least I won't be stranded here.

I look carefully around to make sure no one has taken note of this encounter. There is a woman standing at the front counter picking

118

up bags of takeout food. Her back is to me. Her clothing looks vaguely familiar; and as I scan the room I notice a woman in dark glasses sitting alone at a table in the corner. She seems to be looking my way. I can't really tell who she is, what with the glasses. Someone from St. Swithins'?

Oh, shit. Is that *Peggy*? Of all people. Of all days.

Maybe it isn't. This woman has shorter hair than Peggy did, seems a bit rounder in the face and body. Of course, in a couple of years a person can certainly change.

No. It was more than a couple of years ago. I should recall the date. I just remember it was in the fall, because I raced over the speed limit to her beachfront condo with the car windows down to keep from fainting. There was little humidity. What an odd thing to remember. October? November?

October. Yes. Frankie was four. He insisted over the phone, lisping, that he wanted to come to my house and show me and Grandpa his Batman costume. October 30, that was it. And four years old—that would put it at 2015. Halloween was on a Saturday, and Frankie was going to a little kids' pre-Halloween party on Friday.

Then from nowhere I got a call about three in the afternoon. An unfamiliar woman's voice: "Your husband has had a heart attack. I've called 911."

Not his secretary's voice. The woman gave me an address and directions, along with the gate code, one two three four—I remember thinking what a stupid code that was, that anyone could try it and get in first thing--to a condominium high-rise in a section of north Banana Bay Beach I rarely frequented, repeating it several times while I wrote it down, my hand shaking. No time to even phone Frances, I was so unnerved. I don't know how I found my way—I was too rattled even to enter the address in the car's GPS.

And there was the ambulance. Franklin on a stretcher in a strange driveway. People in uniforms working on him. A woman, rather bosomy, about my age, with obvious home-bleached blonde hair, standing off to the side of the action and clutching a light blue terrycloth bathrobe to her body. An elderly couple holding back a tiny dog with a high-pitched bark, over and over and over. More people standing, staring.

Peggy.

I don't remember if I wished him dead in that moment. I'm sure I didn't, I was so stunned. Now I wonder. I'm ashamed that my first thought was, how dared he embarrass me in this way? And it was worse—one of the ambulance workers was asking the woman in the bathrobe questions as if *she* was Franklin's wife!

She pointed in my direction. I must have looked like a crazed person, my eyes wild, my incomprehension as to what was happening, my trying to get to Franklin and having someone hold me back as they hoisted him into the back of the ambulance.

I had to follow them! But the woman—Peggy, I found out later—grabbed my arm.

"I gave him CPR," she told me in a low voice. An animal scent of recent sweaty lovemaking wafted from her bathrobe. Oh lord, she smelled like Franklin's cologne! "They don't think it was a major heart attack."

I was torn between following the ambulance and dealing with this person first, who continued, "I found your phone number in his wallet. He never would give me his home number—didn't want to chance my calling him there." She seemed to intimate that she and Franklin were both being oh-so-generously thoughtful of me.

She had touched his *wallet!* Franklin had never let me do that.

My innate sense of politeness took over. I must have been in shock. "Thank you," I said.

Those two words, I guess, signaled to her that we were now chums. "They think it was just a mild attack," she said in a buddy-like tone. Oh, so we were to be *friends* now!

"You-- bitch!" was all I could think of to say, now that we had gotten the pleasantries out of the way.

"Look, Maya," she said—I didn't yet know her name, but I remember feeling incensed that she knew mine!—"He'll be okay. This was just unfortunate."

What a thoughtless, careless choice of a word! I sputtered, "Look--just don't *ever* see either of us again!" I don't know where this forcefulness came from. One two three four my rear end.

She surprised me by saying calmly (I heard it as sanctimonious and smug), "I don't think I can promise that without checking first with Franklin."

And that's when I hit her in the face with my Gucci purse, hard enough and unexpectedly enough to make her stagger backwards and sit down hard on her ample rear end. (*"Good!"* I remembered thinking cruelly.) Her bathrobe flew open below its knotted sash and before she had a chance to close it I had a brief unwanted, truly unnecessary view of what had enticed Franklin. Hah—a newly erupted vicious part of me wanted to know when he had first realized she was not a natural blonde like me! Our eyes met for a second or two. She realized, womanlike, exposed, that I knew her fake-platinum hair secret, and it was Lady Clairol.

Of course the second secret was my husband.

A couple of residents who had run outside when they had seen the red lights of the ambulance helped her to her slippered feet ever so gently, as though she was the victim, and not me.

Franklin told me he'd give Peggy up. What else could he say, lying there in a hospital bed, waiting until we were alone while Frances ran out into the hall to find him "something yummy" he'd especially like to eat, Franklin wired up to instruments and me—in public the gracious, understanding me, the wife, in private all of my backwoods West Virginia sense of possessive territorial entitlement leaking from every pore in my body—wanting to rip those caretaking plugs from the walls?

He could read it in my face and I hoped he was chastened, knowing just who would be in charge of him when he came home. It sure as hell would not be Peggy! Just the two of us in our cavernous house together, where I could be as good to him as I cared to be—or not.

Yes, I was that angry back then and my blood was running hot. I saw the way he was keeping the truth of Peggy from Frances, and playing the martyr. It was the first time I felt *above* him, him with all of his Bostonian propriety.

A feeling of God-given superiority plus absolute power—that must be what dictators feel. That was what I felt now. Was Peggy going to be able to phone him? Was he going to be allowed to phone her? Was I going to pick up the mail every day, check his cell phone messages, fire his secretary? Get the den key off his keychain? Drive his car?

Look into his *wallet?*

He must have intuited that I was going to take his life into my hands when he returned home, because I only left him with Frances for the short time it took to get to the nurses' station and order a hospital bed, in case one was needed; and when I got back to his room there was an absolutely *beaming* Frances sitting at the edge of the patient's bed, announcing that Franklin had invited her and Frankie to come move in with us, back into her old room in her old house and out of that dinky apartment! Wouldn't Frankie love it! He could have a *dog*! Dad said he would make it happen!

I watched behind her back as Franklin coughed quietly and grinned at me.

So much for my plan of careful neglect and wifely torture until he acceded to my demand that he never see that awful woman again.

*   *   *

That's what I am thinking, there at the Katz' Meow, knowing that I can't have Franklin declared dead. No, not yet. I need more time to decide, or not decide about this—when someone stops at my table.

I look up. Oh lord, it is indeed Peggy. I can tell it's her, even though she is still wearing dark glasses. I am prideful enough to note that she has gained weight. Up close now I can tell she must be about forty or so years old, although I would judge that she is looking older than that, a woman without access to my Mr. Julian.

It's been a long time coming, but I have been dreaming of the day when I would get to demand an apology from her for fooling around with my husband. She opens her mouth-- the same mouth that had been giving Franklin CPR that fateful day, and very possibly that same mouth on another part of Franklin's that I had never been all that eagerly fond of accommodating—to speak.

Not her turn. I will *not* give her a turn. *Oh, yes, Peggy. Have I got a lot to--!* And then (she looks so dismal, like a Poor Me, rather wilted, no longer a worthy opponent) I surprise myself by interrupting her:

"Peggy, I'm sorry I hit you that day. I took all of my anxiety out on you and if you knew me you would know that I'm really a bigger person than that." Wow. There was all my early Methodist upbringing coming automatically back to me. Judge not, lest ye be judged.

I can tell she is taken aback. "Uh—actually, that's what I came to your table to say to you, that I'm sorry about Franklin and I'm very truly sorry for all you have had to go through this past year." She adds, to my surprise, "You were so distraught back then—I didn't—Franklin told me, but you know husbands—," she stumbles for words, then blurts out, "You're just so *beautiful!*

Was that your daughter with you at lunch just now? The *two* of you--! Were you ever models or--?"

I can't see her eyes, so I can't tell how sincere she is. "Peggy, excuse me. I'm sure you mean well, but I can't talk to you about anything right now."

She stands actually trembling beside my table, across from me. Maybe out of politeness I should ask her to sit down. But before I can decide she asks, "Yes. Of course. Sorry. Uh--do you know anything about Mark Twain's first editions?"

"I beg your pardon--what?"

She looks as though she wants to say something else, opens her mouth, raises a hand (which makes me pull back reflexively), closes her mouth, plucks something from her purse. "Here's my number if you ever need to talk." She sets a card on the table. "If it helps," she says, not smiling, "I want you to know. It wasn't personal against you. I wasn't Franklin's first. And I sure as hell wasn't Franklin's last."

Now it's my turn to be speechless. She moves to leave. Then she turns and actually sits down uninvited in the chair Frances just left. She pushes the half-eaten quiche aside. Her face is somber. "Just so you understand--I'm losing my condo. I don't know where I'll be moving to. I can't afford it on my own."

"You could get yourself a roommate," I say, just to say something. Maybe my tone of voice sounds curt. I'm not sure.

126

She removes her sunglasses to fix me with a long, searching look. Shocked, I see that someone has given her a *very* black eye. Does she have a roommate who did this? Have I said the wrong thing?

"A roommate!" Peggy explodes. "That's a hot one! Yeah, like the bastard I've had all year—a *roommate*!"

She stands up abruptly. "I don't know why Porters keep aiming for my face."

My mind, searching for some sense in all of this, fills in a mental picture of her boarding a train and a couple of porters swinging luggage toward her--.

"--and as far as I'm concerned, " she blurts out in a voice loud enough to make Mrs. Katz come running, "I hope I helped him *ruin* his 'Huckleberry Finn'!"

She walks fast from the restaurant. The front door bangs behind her. Mrs. Katz is left holding Peggy's bill. As I pay it—she just had coffee-- to allay the awkward scene that just took place, I shrink from this insane, albeit brief, encounter. Lordy, lordy, if I'm so beautiful (which others have told me I am)—*then what the hell did Franklin want?*

Apparently from what Peggy just said, he simply wanted what I was reluctant to give him: more playtime with his Huckleberry Finn.

Ten.

Franklin   one year earlier   May 17, 2018
late at night. A calm Atlantic.

I have trouble trusting that people will carry out my orders. I know what I want to do and I don't want to have to explain why to people who weren't paying attention in the first place.

Which is why I had second thoughts about Sherrye, whom I have known for all of twenty-seven nights.

Check out her introduction to me: "Hi there. I'm Sherrye—S-h-e-r-r-y-e--that's two drinks for the price of one. Get it? Sherry and rye. And that's how you pronounce it, too. Oka-ay? I even tried mixing them two drinks together once. What a headache I got! What's your name? Lance? Lance What? Armstrong? Glad to meet you, Lance. Um-m-m. Feel them muscles. Ooh, Lance, you are s-o-o good-lookin'! You here with anybody special or like me, just browsin' an' carousin'?"

You can guess her age pretty much from the spelling of her name. I have spun good old Sher-rye a yarn about we're going to be together forever yada yada yada. Then I gave her a test. It pays to be somewhat paranoid at this point. And not to put too fine a point on it, she's a pretty dim bulb. Which I want: someone with a short memory and just enough attention span.

So. A test drive. Two or so weeks ago we took her nondescript Corolla down A-1-A through Melbourne Beach and south of it, but not as far as Sebastian Inlet. She drove. There was thankfully not much traffic. I pointed out landmarks along the way. She appeared to be listening and taking it all in, *and* able to drive, all at the same time, which made me hopeful.

"Okay, watch, Sherrye, here's this old motel from the fifties on your left. See it?"

"Ooh, there's a gi-normous fishing pole out front with a gi-normous fish on it! That is so *cute*!"

"Right. Now. That would be a landmark to remember, correct?"

"Sure, Lance. Correcto-mundo. What do you take me for?"

"I take you for a beautiful woman who is paying attention to what I am—watch it—you're drifting over to the edge of the road. Are you sure your tires are in good shape?"

"You checked them yourself just last night. Boy, you worry a lot. Me, I just worry about running over a crocodile down here."

"Alligator. Slow down. See that absolutely ugly bright pink mansion—again to your left."

"Uh huh."

"Slow down some more. There's no traffic behind us. Now. Look at that house's mailbox."

"Ooh! It's a great big ole pink flamingo! That's precious!"

"Okay. Now count to three. One, two, three mailboxes beyond, down the road from the flamingo. Still on your left."

"They're kind of far apart."

"They're supposed to be. This is where the multi-rich people from other countries have homes built that they never use."

"What a waste. Lance—do I count the flamingo as one?"

"Brilliant idea. The flamingo is one. Then one, two, three, and—four. Here's where you turn in. Turn here into this driveway and shut off your lights."

"Ooh, it's so dark! Whose house is this?"

"It's a guy's who lives in another country. He won't be back until December, if then."

"What? What's he got a house like this for, then?"

"It's a tax write off."

"Huh."

I have decided not to curse myself for thinking Sherrye could be my lookout. She has actually helped me inadvertently by demonstrating that so many things could go wrong. It's like asking the Marx Brothers to charge San Juan Hill.

"So why are we parked here, Lance? It's creepy."

"I just thought you'd like walking down to the beach."

"Ew-w-w. I don't like getting sand in my shoes."

"Take your shoes off."

"Then I'd get sand in my *car*. Honestly, Lance—"

"Okay. You stay in the car. I'm walking down to the beach."

So I did, with the anguished sounds of Sherrye in the distance shouting, "I think I see a *crocodile*!" fading away. My real reason was to see if there were any people lying on beach towels or walking there.

This was a very dark section of the area on the ocean south of Banana Bay—so many homes the size of entire condominiums, all buttoned up tight with hurricane shutters and electronic surveillance protection against break-ins. All these idiots needed was one major storm surge from a hurricane to wash their foundations out, but that wasn't my concern. I would have even had our home built here, but Maya was too scared of water, since she'd never learned to swim and wasn't about to learn now. It had taken her a while to calm down when I told her I *was* going to have a pool in our backyard, damn it, like she was afraid it was going to develop a tidal wave and engulf her.

131

There were so many holes in this plan where Sherrye was to be my support, holes big enough to drive an Atlas missile through. Well-- as I said earlier, I 'm easily bored. However, this was too important, so I decided to just turn it into a test case. Always play to your strengths, but don't ignore your weaknesses.

As I hoped, the beach was deserted. I looked out to the east, where in a few weeks I would be finalizing my plans on the leakiest boat I was about to buy. Just one mindless catch to the whole thing—Sherrye. I made my way back over the sand dunes to her.

And what a mindless catch she was. What I had to think about right now, sitting in her car that smelled of old takeout food and old past sex, was: would Sherrye make sure she had enough gas in her car? (I'd give her money for that.) Would she take the money and bolt? (It was a chance I had to take.) Would her tires hold out? (Maybe.) Should I rent her a car? (No, for reasons of a paper trail.) Could she remember to count to *four*?

"Lance, honey, let's stop and get a room at that cute old motel with the fishing pole." Damn, Sherrye was fixated on that pole. But I didn't dare. Didn't dare let the manager get a good look at me. So we drove down past Vero instead. She complained about the distance. I told her I'd pay for the gas. I'd already made up my mind not to count on her to help me.

Poor Sherrye—doomed in life to be good at only one thing. But amazingly good at that.

132

Well, we headed back, after she had insulted me by saying that she was sorry, she'd had a good time, but she couldn't see me anymore because, well frankly, I scared her, I was so—

"Intense?" I asked.

"Huh? No, I was gonna say—old. Getting me to count mailboxes like I was a kid."

So that was that. She drove me back to the twenty-four hour CVS pharmacy. Neither one of us had anything left to say. I looked around to determine I hadn't dropped anything incriminating inside her Corolla. I made like I was heading for my car (catch me driving a Fiat!), waiting for her to leave. Then I went to my Mercedes after she was out of sight. She drove off as though she was afraid I was going to change my mind and come running after her.

Then I cruised around for about a half hour, thinking about how I had no friends, no good ones I could rely on except myself and— and one other person, the one who'd already saved my life once! I almost slapped my head with my open palm, the way cartoon characters do. It was very late, but what did I care? I needed—she hadn't changed the gate code. One two three four. Now *here* was a woman who could count mailboxes. I rang the doorbell. It didn't even occur to me that she might be with someone else. I knew she wasn't that kind of person.

I could see it in her face, which lit up like the neon at an all-night gas station, when she saw me. Now *here* was someone with a brain, someone who would remember my orders, someone who would keep her mouth shut unless it was on *my* mouth—

She kissed me a deep kiss, the kind I never got from Maya, and I knew I was right.

"Hey there, Peggy."

*   *   *

It's a calm night here on the Atlantic. If there were a full moon (which it is not—I made very careful plans), it would be reflecting like mad off this still water. I've already seen some porpoises, which is always a good sign that there are no sharks around—I don't know why. Porpoises always look as though they're laughing and sharks never do. Sharks have no sense of humor. Just killing machines. Don't think that right now, Porter.

If I've prepared everything correctly, I'll have time to get the Styrofoam cooler into the water and me with it, and I'll push it toward shore until I'm fairly sure it will float the rest of the way. If the Coast Guard is alerted to come find me, I'm not sure they'd see a little cooler bobbing in the ocean. That's a chance I'll have to take, that someone will find it. My will's already at home in my den, so that's taken care of.

Time to get dressed for The Big Moment. I'll need to stay warm while I'm in the water. I haven't been able to test this outfit. Worried that Maya would ask questions. She sure changed after my heart attack. Great idea I had, sending her off to that week end course in Orlando so I could sneak away for time with Peggy. Hated to lie to Frances, but as Jack Nicholson said, She couldn't have handled the truth.

Goggles too, to keep the salt out of my eyes. Flippers for my feet. Oof—how do women wear girdles? But I can feel I'm already warmer. Whole body covered except for my nose. I consider the snorkel, then reject it. Then decide to take it. The Man in Black.

I'm in the water maybe a couple thousand yards from the boat, feeling oh so confident and alive, being my own man, heading for shore—it's hard to judge the distance—when suddenly there's a "BOOM!" and "whoomp" I feel some heat at the back of my head. I turn and there it is on the horizon, doing just what I'd planned for it to do, billowing black smoke. Maybe the explosion has scared off sharks, too.

The water, as I've already noted, is calm and not too cold, as outfitted as I am, and I'm rather tired already of this cooler that I'm lugging along with me. I'm using it to hold onto and rest with when I need to, but maybe this was not such a good idea. I may be using up more energy hanging onto it than letting it go.

I have a moment of panic when the clouds hide the sliver of moon and I wonder if I have not turned myself around and am heading out for wide-open water; but then the clouds part and there's that tiny silver ribbon up there helping me to guide me to shore and now, unless I'm kidding myself, I can barely make out some scattered dots of light—the shoreline. Huzzah!

I'm an excellent swimmer—I've been practicing a lot at home in my lap pool. I've gotten well past the fear that I'll have another heart attack. *Then* that stupid diagnosis of cancer, which turned out to be wrong, wrong, wrong and which impelled me into this plan.

Nothing like a little life and death scare to give a man religion. That, plus hoodwinking Rocco out of a shitload of money.

Good-by, cooler. I've had enough of you. Go float your way to the beach. You were a real hindrance.

You reminded me of Maya.

Damn, I'm getting thirsty now. Franklin, old boy, don't dwell on that. Just a little to go. Remember we have a plan! And it's easier to swim now with the cooler gone.

Those guys at the docks in South Carolina when I was stocking my new boat—I don't know, don't all guys around the docks in every city look a little Mafioso-ish, a little like Rocco? Maybe,

136

but I wouldn't put it past them for following me. Get out while you can, that's my motto with thugs and women and sex. I'll tell you, Franklin, old bean, I'm really getting jazzed about dyeing my hair and growing a beard. Always wanted a beard. Maya hated them. I tried one once. Couldn't get past the scraggly stage because of her. She said when I kissed her it was like sandpaper.

Wish I'd kept a list. That one could be number three-oh-two of "Maya's Reasons Not To Kiss Franklin". Garlic, onions, beer, vodka, cheese, an occasional cigar, so forth and so on, all those manly things. She think those West Virginny boys smelled like peaches and clover?

Wait. There's a ripple ahead in the water. Careful. Sharks can smell fear. All my best-laid plans and then to lose them all at the whim of some dumb-ass shark. Come on, Franklin. Breathe. Go calm.

Porpoises! Oh, my new buddies, my seaworthy bodyguards! *I love you all!*

Suddenly I think I see a tiny duo of lights flash-flash, but this can't be true. I don't think I've been swimming for a long enough time. I turn onto my back and float for a bit. When I turn over, there's a flash-flash of light again, a little bigger than before. I must be closer than I thought. As the poet (the real one, not Maya) says: "My heart soars".

I take a look around to see how fast my cooler is drifting toward shore, but the night is black enough that I can't even see a piece of white in the water.

Now the next problem: will there be any people on the beach tonight near my out-of-the-country client's mansion? I've been stymied by the amount of things I can't control, but again, second-guessing, stepping carefully is not part of my makeup. What say, Father? Look where your swimming-champ son is tonight.

I'm starting to breathe a little harder now. Own up, Porter. No longer a college kid, eh, Porter? Could be worse: you could be a smoker. That was an irritating aspect of Sherrye—she smoked. Now *Peggy*—there's that flash-flash again, a bit brighter now, but to my right, where it was to my left the last time. The current is shoving me to the south.

Gotta take these flippers off. Wish I'd thought of socks or something—the friction is hurting my ankles like hell and it won't do any good at this point to make my feet bleed. Sharks come up to Banana Bay Beach in shallow water.

Saw one caught once, right near where I'm hoping to come ashore. Kids saw it first, started yelling. A fisherman came along, cast his line out and caught it, dragged it to shore. A couple dozen people in bathing suits watched as silent as if they were at a golf tournament; and when the shark finally lay gasping its last on the sand, they all applauded politely at the fisherman's watery hole in one.

Thanks, Porter. You're full of cheer, you are.

I wiggle my toes. Gonna have blisters. Over on my back again with my freed-up feet, for just a moment.

Will you look at all those goddamned stars! Each one could be growing a world like ours. What a dismal thought. Lord, we screwed this one up badly enough to kill it off, mostly since Your kid was born—was this then Your noble Plan all along—give us all brains so's we could invent ways to kill each other off?

I wish *I'd* had a son. Even so, I treated my gorgeous Frances like the son I never had. Gave her as much of my name as I could. God, I'll miss her more than anyone! I can't *believe* the money I spent to hunt her creep of an ex-husband down and threaten him with instant death if he ever got in touch with her or Frankie again.

I'll bet *my* father wishes he'd had a daughter instead of me. . . . "What dreams may come"—did Shakespeare lie under the stars like this—did he float in the Avon and get the inspiration for his best lines? Funny to think of him looking at these same stars.

Stars—Liz Taylor. Now *there's* a Star. One of my role models is Mike Todd, the film impresario, one of her husbands, I forget which number. Doesn't matter. He invented a wide screen called-- uh—oh yeah, "Todd A-O". Millionaire. Then he accidentally—I guess it was an accident—who'd want to leave Liz Taylor?--crashed a plane into a mountain. He said what has become my watchword: "I've been broke, but I've never been poor". Good for you, Mike baby. Good for you. . . .

Maybe when people die *they* become stars.

Do we live again, go through all this shit again? Come back as someone else?

If so, I want to come back as a mosquito on Rocco's butt. Huh. That's a riot, considering all the cash I drained out of him, now sitting in a bank on the other coast just waiting for me. . . .

Enough putzing around. How long have I been drifting here? Did I drift off, fall asleep like a truck driver on the road too long? *Drift off.* That's funny, considering my situation. "I'm reviewing/The situation"—great song. I could identify with Fagin, except I never liked kids that much.

Wake up. Wake up. Back to some serious swimming. Go toward the light, as the woman in that exorcism movie with the little girl said. I am, lady, I am. Spielberg—didn't he do that one? And he did the one about the giant shark, too. Shut up, Porter.

I'm cold, now, I can feel the cold, and my swimming pace has slowed down. Three miles—maybe the boat wasn't all of three miles out—even so, that's a long way to swim, even in salt water. I am so thirsty. I hope Peggy brought water for me. That's another great thing about her—her mind.

Whoa! Was that--?

My foot scrapes against something and I shudder and recoil automatically—coquina rock! I'm close to shore! Very sharp stuff. Got to be careful now. It wouldn't do me any good to get scraped up and infected, this close to total success.

And there's the flash-flash so close I could hug it. The last wave helps to deposit me on shore as smoothly as if I were a baby being put to bed. I lie on my stomach on the beach and pant as quietly as I can. Then I raise my head and look around ever-so-carefully, listening for that most unwelcome sound: a twosome in heat making love on a blanket nearby; but all I hear are cicadas in the twisted wild grape bushes almost above my head. I can't even hear any cars going by on A-1-A. The beach and dunes are so steep and carved out here, all the way up to the driveway, that people would be more inclined to find some other beach without an incline.

I laugh silently at my joke. So very far, so very good! Tah-dah! I am about to pull the ultimate disappearing act. With good old reliable Peggy.

The sand is cool without the sunshine on it. It's an otherworldly sensation—sand is supposed to be *hot*. Hey. Don't drop the snorkel, Porter. You'll never find it in the dark, not that it matters now. Anybody picking it up would just think some kid had lost it.

Bon voyage, cooler. I wonder where *you* ended up.

Eleven.

Maya   2:15 pm   May 17, 2019
Banana Bay Mall

<u>Even a Sparrow</u>   a poem by Maya Porter   2015

Still I sat on the weathered steps

Leading down to the surf

And fretted about my future.

Two dusky sparrows flew near and perched. One

Fluttered off. Its companion

Bobbed on the wood close to me, as if

Weighing the consequences of staying or not.

So I helped it by stirring slightly

And the sparrow, unsettled

Flew away.

Even a sparrow must decide yes or no

And while it was deciding, I got in its way.

I gave it something to do.

I gave myself something to do.

*   *   *

A sensible woman still can't go on her own to a bar in the middle of the day. At least that's my belief. I've never checked it out.

But I can tell you one place that's safe for a female to sit and spill her secrets, if she chooses.

Mr. Lu holds my left foot in his hands and gently adds it to the right one in the warm swirling water. I sit like a princess above his lowered head thick with dark hair. He is ready to do my bidding. He smiles up at me even when he doesn't understand me—this language barrier, this Tower of Babel--.

"So now," Mr. Lu asks, "Cullah?"

I have such trouble deciding on the right color for my toes that I always get a neutral one. But the words that Peggy and I exchanged have left me shaken, so I say, "You choose this time, Mr. Lu. I won't even peek!"

He nods, looking pleased, and I close my eyes. I know a little of his past—he and his family were persecuted for their Catholic faith. Imagine. I thought all Vietnamese were Buddhists. That's how much I know. They left Viet Nam before they could be tortured and killed. He and his wife and their toddler escaped with only two bags of possessions: one bag of clothing for the child and one of food for the child. Every time I think of all that I have, I want to make amends somehow. I had more in West Virginia than they ran away with!

Unbidden, the image of the peregrine falcon enters my mind. Why, they have these birds in Viet Nam as well as here! "Peregrine" means "wanderer" and these falcons have wandered everywhere on the globe, even to Mr. Lu's home in Viet Nam.

Frankie was given a brochure at the bird sanctuary. He read it to me in the car on our way home, watching to see if my face would squint: "Peregrines are very clean birds. They spend a lot of time searching for shallow water, to clean the lice and blood from themselves. This seems rather gory, but to avoid mentioning it would be to ignore this bird's nature. They are, after all, meat eaters, seeking warm-blooded birds and animals as their prey.

"When farmers were using pesticides for their plants, they were unaware for years that they were also dec-dec-decimating the falcon population. The poisoned peregrines would fall on their backs dead from up in the sky. Also, when the females laid eggs, the shells would be so thin from the birds' diet that included the pesticides, that the baby birds were doomed from the very beginning.

"The peregrine population almost died out completely until the farmers became aware of the dangers of the pesticides and began using other kinds of bug sprays. The peregrine population was saved and has returned to its former numbers."

He turned to me. I had indeed found the "lice and blood" sentence yucky. "Maya, what does 'decimate' mean?"

"It means 'killing off'," I replied, my eyes on the traffic. I didn't tell him that once I looked up the word "kill" in my Thesaurus— my prize for my prize-winning poem in high school-- to find that the book had an *entire page* devoted to synonyms for that word. So many! Alive and breathing one moment, dead the next. Why would so many words be needed for that?

"So, the *owls* decimated the *mice* in the new houses!"

"Right you are, my man."

"Maya. I still like the owls better than that falcon or that turkey buzzard or any of the other birds. Miss Betsy said that screech owls have three eyelids! And barn owls have twenty-three different calls, but no hoot."

"Goodness. How do you remember all those things?"

Decimated—that's what our soldiers were doing to Mr. Lu's country with Agent Orange. Why would human beings do that to other human beings? And why water down the act, to spin it, with so many synonyms?

I recently met a woman named Mary, also from Viet Nam. She was in my very first "No More Poor Me!" class. She brought me tomatoes from her garden, the best tomatoes I had ever eaten. She told me she had come to this country and had gone to school to become an engineer. Again I had been humbled by the opportunities here that I had not taken advantage of.

Oh, I tried going back to college, to the local community one here in Banana Bay, but of course there was Frances and then there was the house and my poem writing, of course—and somehow the years went by. Oh, and civic and social duties as Franklin's wife. Those took up a lot of time.

"We lived underground in caves while the fighting was going on," Mary told me in a quiet voice, still a hint of accent in her whispery words so that I had to lean closer to hear her.

"Underground? For how long?" I can't believe this. While our troops were there!

"Seven, eight years."

"Mr. Lu," I ask, still with my eyes closed, "did you know of anyone in your country who lived in caves?"

"Yes," he says shortly. "We not talk about these things." He pauses. "Like cullah?"

I open my eyes. I wiggle my toes, which are now clean, white, perfectly pedicured, and—bright blue-green!

"Cullah?"

"Oh—yes. Oh, my. It's just--I've never worn—this color before."

"Matches dress. You say next time: 'Ocean Wattah'. "

He holds a bottle of nail polish before my eyes. Ocean Water. It is indeed. I can't help myself—I laugh. What a perfectly ironic color for an ironic anniversary.

"Good?" Mr. Lu's face waits for my approval.

"Good. Yes. Good. Yes. Um-- Mr. Lu—I'm sorry we fought on your soil, in your land."

"Ah. Yes. So many have fought in our land, for so many thousands years. United States one of many."

I marvel that he could come to a place that had invaded his homeland, setting his native land on fire, wasting its beauty, all in the name of—what? I was barely born when all of this was happening, but I still feel a need to atone somehow. Just giving Mr. Lu a tip as thanks seems paltry. I imagine his country looked much the same as my country of West Virginia.

"Mr. Lu?"

He looks at me. There is such kindness in his eyes after what I just went through with first Frances and then Peggy, at lunch. "Mr. Lu—mountains in your country?" I roll my hands up and down in waves to emphasize my words.

"Ah. Mountains. Beautiful green mountains. You go see."

"I'd like to. Do—do you ever go back there?"

His face has closed down, either from remembering or from wanting not to remember. I'm sorry if I have given him any painful thoughts. I'd like to ask him what his occupation was in his country, but I'm reluctant to. What if he said he was a doctor once and now here he is, washing people's feet?

The thought of having to live in a cave—I'd once walked a ways into an old abandoned mining cave and it had *scared* me--! Bats had flown over my head and I had run screaming out, terrified, while the ten-year-old schoolmate who had dared me into the cave as a prank had laughed his fool head off.

I bow my head. "Thank you, Mr. Lu. An honor." He bows and turns to his next customer. "Ah. Miss Sherrye. Please to sit."

Funny the way he pronounces that name, like it's "Share Eye". Share an eye.

The young woman and I share an eye—a casual nonchalant glance, the kind you give to a stranger. And I am back out in the sunlight, reaching for my sunglasses. Sunglasses—Peggy.

An eye for an eye. What a terrible saying. The peregrine and its stare—it should have been a heartless look, dispassionate, a merciless one, just that of a bird on the wing, a killing mechanism for smaller creatures. Instead, it seemed to see right through me, as though the bird was reaching into my soul.

(we survived   as do you   you are worthy   worth much
fly   fly

Twelve.

Maya   3:15 pm   May 17, 2019   Maya's home

<u>Circles</u>   a poem by Maya Porter   2016

When she was young our infant daughter

Moved in circles which did not stretch

Beyond the full moon of the breast

And the island of the crib.

At her command and she to mine

I enlarged her realm.

Am I then only a protesting pool-tossed pebble

Whose circles, newly formed,

Thank their pebble-mother for their existence

With one brief watery kiss

Before rippling away to cause

Sun-splintered rainbows

Without ever returning?

The drowning stone, its purpose served,

Dares not assume her circles

 Will ever have a homecoming.

I must assume mine will.

           *   *   *

I have just time to arrive home, come in through the garage, see that Frankie's bike is safely against the wall and not against Franklin's Mercedes, meaning that Frankie is home from school, check the air conditioner temperature, hear Frankie's tv set blasting away, call out, "Frances? Frankie?" and set my purse down, when there is a loud banging at our (mostly unused) front door. I note as I walk past the phone on the kitchen counter, that its answerphone light is blinking. *Franklin?* I think hopefully, as I have all this past year.

I can't stop and check. The pounding continues. And now the bell. The front door, used only a few times this past year, sticks when I open it. On the other side of the door stands an unfamiliar young woman, probably in her early thirties. Her eyes are blazing and her hair is a mess. Her glasses have fingerprints all over the lenses. *It must be hard for her to see*, I think. She looks like a demented salesperson for Jesus. I step back, my hand holding tight to the door handle.

"Where is he? What have you done with him?" she demands.

"Who?" (My god, is this yet another version of Peggy?)

"My son! My son!"

"Uh—you must have the wrong—"

 "My son!-- is Dean Holcomb. He is in your grandson Frankie's class, and according to his teacher, he was sent to your nurses' station this morning and he never returned to his class."

"Well—how nice to meet you—"

"His teacher didn't worry until I came to his room to get him to take him to his piano lesson and she then realized she hadn't seen him return to his desk."

"Well, that's because—that's because—"

152

"So where is my son? You were the last to see him!"

"Oh. Please come in, Mrs. Holcomb. I'm Maya Porter."

"Sandra. I *know* who you are. From the papers and the tv. My son, please!"

She is frantic, I can tell. "May I get you some water?"

My calmness apparently radiates to her a bit. "Here. Please sit. I'll get you some water and I'll go check with Frankie. The boys are probably just playing together."

I seat Sandra Holcomb in an occasional chair in the living room, get her a glass of water (I don't know her at all well enough to ask if I may clean her lenses for her), and I walk back toward Frankie's room. I can hear him on the house phone extension. He is yelling, "No, *you're* the oofie!" and laughing uproariously, as though someone has tickled him.

"Frankie," I say, and he again says to the person at the other end of the line, "No, I said it first—*you're the oofie!*"

"Frankie!" He looks up. "Hang on," he says and waits, trying not to laugh.

"Frankie, do you know where Dean is?"

"Deano the Beano!" he shouts. "Deano the Beano! Doofie the Oofie!"

"Frankie—"

He looks at me and raises both his voice and his eyebrows. "Maya! Maya, Deano says the puppies are getting big enough to—"

"Frankie, stop. Stop. No puppies right now. I just want to know if you know where Dean is."

His face shuts itself into a mask of stubbornness. "I really, really, *really* want a dog."

"I know that, Frankie, but—"

"You said that we—Maya, you tricked me! You said my report was a good one!"

"Well, of course. It was excellent!"

"My teacher *hated* my report about the birds."

"Oh, no!"

"She said why didn't I do what the rest of the class did and write about the rocket shot?"

"Well—were you supposed to?"

"I guess. Maybe. I don't know. But she hated my bird one!"

The doorbell rings. "I'll be right back," I say, as I head for the front of the house. Oh, where is Frances? She should be straightening all this out. I can hear Frankie back on the phone, back to his "oofie" friend.

Sandra has taken the liberty of opening my front door and to my astonishment there stands the elementary school principal, Mrs. Stewart.

"May I come in, Mrs. Porter?" she asks, pushing her way in as she says so. She is a large woman—the polite word is "stout"—and she regards, with no sense of humor whatsoever, her station at the school as permission to run things her way. I really feel intimidated by her. I catch her arm so that she won't miss the step going down into the living room and she glares at my taking such a liberty with her.

"We are seeking the whereabouts of young Dean Holcomb," she says. "You were the last to see him, I believe."

Sandra is now sniffling into a tissue.

"Oh!" I say in relief. "No, I wasn't the last one. My grandson Frankie was."

"And how did this come about?"

"Well, Frankie brought Dean into the nurses' room. See, Dean was complaining of his stomach hurting—"

"Of course it was!" Sandra Holcomb bursts out. "Call yourself a nurse? He was constipated! His father does that to him every week, feeding him junk food and then *I* have to pay the consequences!"

I privately think that it's *Dean's* insides that are paying here, but—

"Anyway, he said he wanted to go home and he lived across the street from the school, and Frankie said he'd watch to make sure Dean got across the street all right. And then--," I rack my brain. So much has happened today! "Oh, then Frankie said that Dean had a key to the house and he said that Dean went inside and shut the door, and I was busy with Jessica and her bloody nose, and—"

"You did not sign him out," thunders Mrs. Stewart.

"What? Oh, I guess I didn't. As I said, I was busy—"

"There was not even an entry with young Dean's name on it—not the time, not the complaint, not the procedure used."

"I want charges brought against this woman!" Sandra shrieks. She has been snorting and looking rather desperately around the room like a cornered wild hog. To my horror I see her eyeing Franklin's collections of rare Ming porcelain pieces that I'm so careful to dust. She is upset enough, I fear, to sweep them all off the coffee table with one flailing blow.

"*Charges*? But I told you—!"

"That will come later, I assure you." Mrs. Stewart holds up a hand like a traffic cop. Sandra, spent for the moment, sits back down. She is now staring at my blue-green toenails. If she were a cartoon character her pupils would be spinning like pinwheels, I think.

"Mrs. Porter!" Apparently my mind has wandered.

"But, Mrs. Stewart, I don't understand—charges?"

Mrs. Stewart stands as though at a podium. "You have *lost* this woman's child, Mrs. Porter."

At this Sandra wails, "We have to call the police!"

I am stunned. I *have* lost a child, a child in my keeping. What could I have been thinking?

And miraculously at the doorway from the family room appears my savior. Frances.

"What's going on?" she asks. "Hi, Sandra. Mrs. Stewart." We three women talk at once. Frances frowns, immediately understanding that her son is somehow involved. "Frankie!" she calls.

There is a moment of silent anticipation and Frankie appears, scraping his sneakered feet against the carpet as if to slow himself down from what is to come. He looks guarded and his demeanor changes to one of defensiveness when he sees his principal and his friend's mother. He hugs himself against Frances, who puts her hand on his head.

"Frankie, we're looking for Dean."

"Why?" he says.

"He's missing."

"How?"

"We don't know how. And we don't know where he is. Do you know? You were the last one to see him."

"He went home." Frankie mumbles. He is, to my mind, hiding something.

"And then where?" Mrs. Stewart demands.

"Well. My *Grandma* said it was okay. *Grandma*, you did, didn't you?"

Uh-oh. He's up to something. He's never been given permission to call me by that name. I suspect he's about to bargain like a kidnapper for Dean's release. And a dog.

"Frankie," his mother reminds him, "you are supposed to call her Maya, remember?"

Frankie is silent.

"Franklin, I must insist—," this from Mrs. Stewart.

"Please allow me to question my own child, Mrs. Stewart."

I've never seen Frances like this! She could lose her job—Mrs. Stewart, like an evil-eyed octopus, has tentacles attached to all the schools, and yet Frances is being so stalwart. She rumples her son's hair.

"Frankie," says Sandra Holcomb, calmer now that Frances has taken some of the charged electricity from the air, "just tell me if you know where Dean is."

Frankie is looking down. "Not sure," he mutters.

"Well, do you know where he *was*?"

"At his house."

Mrs. Stewart chuffs. Not only an octopus but an angry bull! This is a woman who, I imagine, is used to getting to the bottom of things and knows that time is money and we are all wasting hers. "Franklin, I am going to count to three—."

Out-finessed, the boy blurts, "I *know* he was home. Now he's not. I don't know for sure where he is!"

"I just *know* he's been kidnapped!" Sandra cries out. Frankie's eyes widen.

"And how, Franklin, do you know he is not at home?" Oh, Mrs. Stewart is relentless. I would have given him a cookie as incentive. She has undoubtedly had much experience interrogating children, who I'll bet all wet their pants answering her.

" 'cause-- he called me."

"Yes? And from where?"

"A car phone."

159

"A car? He's in a *car*?" Sandra is getting herself pretty worked up, I fear. But I would too, if I couldn't find Frankie. Now a bolt of terror hits me: Dean has been kidnapped and they tried to get Frankie, too, but he got out of the car in time--!

"Yes? Franklin? And whose car phone?"

"He—didn't tell me. He was just playing with it and fooling around and we called each other oofies, stuff like that!"

Sandra Holcomb yells, "My god! *Do* something! My son *has* been kidnapped!"

Frances does. She gets down on one knee and says softly and surprisingly, "You really want us to move to our own place? You really want a puppy?"

He grabs her around the neck. "Oh, Mom!" It's a cry of hope and desperation mixed. I should be thinking only of Dean and my standing in the community if all this goes public and I'm hauled into court on the very anniversary day of Franklin's disappearance, but I am really more than a little put out that my grandson would be so happy to leave me.

Someone else rings the doorbell, a long and piercing ring. Frankie beats us to the door, opening it wide, and there, sticking his tongue out at Frankie, is—Dean. Deano the Beano. "Oofie, oofie—you're the oofie!!" shouts Dean, as he jabs a fist into Frankie's chest.

"Dean!" screams Sandra Holcomb, knocking over her water glass in her rush to get to her son, who looks confused. Mrs. Stewart frowns. Frances moves to clean up the spill so efficiently that I am the only one who notices.

And there is yet *another* woman entering our house behind theTiggerish Dean. I am once again at a loss—it's Amanda from my class! The unruffled Amanda who is able to ruffle me. How did she get Dean away from his kidnapper?

"What's up?" she says. "Frances, Mrs. Stewart. Looks like a tea party."

She gives me that knowing look again. "Maya, listen. Sorry I didn't get to say hello at lunch today."

She's not at all sorry, her look says. Oh, no—she spotted me with Peggy. She must have eavesdropped on our conversation. "Oh. Were you at lunch? I didn't see you."

"Obviously." She moves to Sandra Holcomb's side. "Yuck. Don't you ever clean your glasses? Listen—I went to your house to take you to lunch and this kid was there all by himself, eating peanut butter out of the jar with his fingers, refrigerator door wide open. You know. So we fed the dog and Dean said he'd leave you a note—"

"Oh, yeah, Mom. I forgot."

"Dean!" The boy looks unrepentant.

161

"So I took the kiddo here to lunch and a movie—"

I can't help myself. I butt in, "I didn't see you or Dean at the Katz's!"

"Maya, I didn't say I *ate* there. I said I didn't get to say hello, because I picked up lunch to go and meet my friend—"

"Boy, she had a totally huge black eye, Mom!"

"—my friend *Peggy.*"

Yes, Amanda, I think. I have figured it out, thank you, Amanda.

"So Dean and I ate our lunches at Peggy's and Peggy just talked and talked. We never did get to a movie. Peggy has a couple of Siamese cats and you know how I love those."

"Wow, we were way up high looking at the ocean. Can we move there, Mom? Can we? Miss Peggy says she's selling her place. We could move there!"

"Uh-uh! Mom! *We* could move there!" This from Frankie. My life is unraveling in my living room full of women and children. All at once I realize: this room has *never* been full of women or children. Just Franklin's cronies. No one looks comfortable, I note. This is not a room built for comfort. No wonder that damned Sofa fits right in. No wonder I thought of Franklin somehow when I bought it.

This is, I understand for the first time, a house built for Franklin and show, not for me.

162

(the peregrine stares at me   do it   do it   fly)

"No, 'cause you're the oofie!" Dean moves to the white Sofa to sit down. "Sorry—Maya is returning this," Frances says, smoothly moving the boy into the kitchen. "A snack for you two guys?" she asks. "Wash your hands first."

Amanda sits down on the Sofa. No inattentive fool she, she smiles an insider's smile. She holds up her hands, palms toward me, so that I can see they are clean. Now I'm really scared of her: the Sofa seems to like her.

Suddenly this from Mrs. Stewart: "Mrs. Holcomb? Didn't you think to call your sister, to see if she might have seen your son?"

Sister? Huh. I am seeing now the resemblance between the other two women in my living room.

Amanda opens her purse and retrieves her cell phone. She taps it, and there is Sandra's voice, over and over, at least a half dozen messages, each one a little more frantic: "Hey, where are you? Looking for Dean. You got him? Call me. Bye."

Mrs. Stewart scans the room for someone, anyone, to blame. "Mrs. Holcomb, do you have anything else to say to Mrs. Porter?"

"Well, I guess—no. It's all okay."

163

"However, Mrs. Stewart, I think this is a wake-up call that the volunteers in charge of the nurses' station need a workshop on how to address situations like this."

Wow. Amanda has beat Mrs. Stewart to the punch. And she used all the buzzwords of Principal-speak. I have to admire her for it.

So I need to speak up while everyone is looking less litigious: "Mrs. Stewart, Sandra, I want to apologize. I did not understand protocol, but that is no excuse. I will not serve as a nurse from here on. Amanda has made a good point." Oh, what it costs me to say that last sentence! But if I'm teaching people about "Poor Me", I cannot afford to be one myself. And I'm certainly feeling like one right now.

"Will you write it up and schedule a workshop, Amanda?" Mrs. Stewart wants everything shipshape as soon as possible. The school kids must run in the opposite direction when they see her coming. I know I would. Unsmiling, she trains her eye on me.

"Mrs. Porter, I am granting you some leeway, considering what an ill-advised day this is for you." I take this as a kind of apology from the school principal and I nod primly. "Amanda?"

"Of course, Mrs. Stewart. Consider it done." Mrs. Stewart nods at Amanda and then looks at me: *you see, that's how to get things accomplished!* My little classroom teachings seem so—amateurish!—next to these two people. How organized they appear. I'll bet they could dash off a sonnet while changing their shoes.

Sandra Holcomb has drifted away to the far end of the house as if afraid to lose her son again, or else to use him as an excuse to do some snooping. I see Mrs. Stewart ("Well, no harm's done!" she has told me rather reluctantly. I already know that I will never be asked to volunteer again) to the door.

Amanda, to my surprise, lingers. She has taken a book from Franklin's shelves and is reading its title page. She turns to me. "You have an interesting collection of books here, Maya. I noticed some first editions, like this one."

"They're all Franklin's."

"You really should have them appraised. They must be quite valuable."

"Oh, I couldn't. When Franklin returns—"

Now she appraises *me*. "You really are convinced that he's coming back, aren't you?"

"What—may I ask what Peggy's opinion of that was?" Oh, I am so bold! Ordinarily I would not want to know another's take on things, especially Peggy's.

"To tell the truth, she has never talked about him with me and we've been friends for a long time. Oh, I know *now,* after the CPR incident, about her affair with your husband. I don't think anyone else does. She was circumspect. Actually, she could work for the CIA, the way she knows how to keep secrets. I certainly didn't have a clue, and she's my best friend. *You* didn't know, did you? Not until she phoned you that day. I gather she saved his life."

She probably did save his life! I am stunned. I had only been thinking about my response, not about Franklin. I should have thanked her and what did I do instead? Hit her with my purse. My face reddens.

"I am enjoying your class, Maya. "

"Really?"

"Yes. You have such a unique take on matters. And you are kind to your students."

"Well—thanks."

"I miss your poems."

"My—my poems?"

"You used to write them for the newspaper. They were interesting. Touching. Quite revealing. I wonder why you gave up doing them."

"Oh. Well—last year, you know--."

"Will you mind if I say something about them, Maya?"

'No. Of course not." Actually, of course I mind. Especially from Amanda. I steel myself for criticism.

"You seem to write two different styles of poems, I've observed. When you write the ones that *rhyme,* it's almost as if you're trying too hard, trying to get an audience to approve of you. But then it's as if you are rather bound by the words. But when you let go the need to rhyme and just go for the mood, the colors, your emotional involvement—then the poems are looser, freer. They fly. You wrote one about circles, about letting our kids go, that I thought was spot-on. Right?"

"You really think my poems-- fly?"

"Yes. They soar. Like they're let loose, as I said. Something like that. And some have an unexpected sadness in the last lines. I hope I haven't upset you." She moves to the piano and sits. "May I?"

"Uh—you play?" In response she dashes off a piece of a popular song, in a rather plaintive jazzy way. Her long lacquered fingers seem to caress the poor neglected keys.

I applaud despite myself, captivated, free of Mrs. Stewart. Amanda rises, pushes the bench carefully back underneath the piano, lowers the lid. I get her meaning—she will not take advantage of the moment.

"You know that song, Maya? Sure you do. 'In the Still of the Night.' Cole Porter." She actually gives me a light fist bump on my arm. "Hell-o? 'Porter'? Guess he's some distant relative of Franklin's."

There's that wry kind of smile from her again. Something's not quite right here. She seems to be acting a little too familiar. I move slightly away from her.

"Needs tuning," she says.

"Nobody here knows how to play it," I say.

"Pity. It's a very good Yamaha. Works better when it's played often." There's that look again. Is she toying with me? Double entendres? That's it!—that's what she does. And then if you guess it correctly, she denies that was what she meant.

"Well. I'm off. Lovely sofa, by the way. Comfy." She gives It a pat on the arm and I come very close to pleading with her to take It; but I am saving It for Franklin.

It's as if she knows my plan. "You are such a fortunate woman, Maya. So many opportunities. I'm still looking for mine."

(the peregrine in an angry frenzy beats its wings at me   come fly   fly)

But I'm ignoring the peregrine right now. A distasteful idea has wormed itself into my head: Franklin has had an affair with

168

Amanda! Now I'm regarding her in a different light, the sultry way she sat on the Sofa, the sensuous way she fingered Franklin's books and his piano, those damned double meanings--!

"Ah, Maya, I hate to think of your spending your life waiting for someone who is not going to walk through that front door. Apologies for sounding out of line, of course."

I don't know how to respond. She calls out, "Sandra! I'm leaving. 'Bye, Dean honey!" There is no response. She turns back to me. "Probably can't hear me. You can let them know. And Frances and Frankie. Nice color on the nails, too. Mr. Lu?"

"Oh. Yes. Ocean Water."

"So appropriate. See you at church." A fast unexpected kiss on my mouth. She is gone. I close the front door behind here. I shove my hands into my pockets and my fingers feel a card in one. I pull out Peggy's card.

"Maya!" Frances calls me. I absently drop the card onto the table beside the phone.

I find the group in Frankie's room. He is reading them his report, I see, noting the blue folder in his hands. Probably his mother's idea. He closes it to applause.

"Mom, we gotta go to that bird place!" Dean shouts. "When can we go?"

I wonder how many children spend their early lives asking, "When can we go? When can we go home? When can we have supper? When can I be big enough to drive? Go on that Disney ride? Wear makeup? Stay out later at night?" They really have so little say in their lives. And when they finally get those things—what then? Happiness? Fruition? What were they hurrying toward? Oh, life is such a puzzle!

(*life is no puzzle* *life is responding to our own unbridled call* *we must fly*)

"Frankie, listen. Your teacher--I'm going to talk with her to see what happened."

"I liked that report, too, Frankie," I add. Sandra nods in agreement, but I can see she has not yet forgiven me for losing Dean.

"I've--Frankie, I've been thinking about that peregrine falcon a lot since we met her." That's not quite true: she has been crowding into my thoughts all day today since Frankie read his report to me this morning. She has been shoving at me, prodding me, her eyes as huge and mystical as the light-filled paintings of the Renaissance visionaries.

"If I was *big*," Frankie muses, "I'd *break* into that place at night and let that bird go!"

"How come?" I ask. A little kid's wish. And mine.

He's apparently thought about this. "Because birds should be able to make up their own minds. *This* way, Miss Betsy is deciding *for* her. And that's not right."

"An interesting point," I say, impressed with his thinking.

"Miss Betsy was just *pretending* she knew! She's not *God*!" helps Dean. "Only *God* can tell that bird to fly or not fly!"

Huh. I wonder what church they attend. Certainly not St. Swithins', not with that predestination-leaning point of view. With that kind of reasoning God gave those boys the bb guns.

"Come on." Sandra gets up. "I have to go feed Big Mama. My lesbian sister still here?" I blink. *Really*? She nods toward Dean. "Oh, don't worry. He knows."

Dean indeed does know. "Yeah. She likes girlfriends better than boyfriends." He and Frankie both mock-shudder together. "Yuck. Can't stand *girls.* " They pretend to gag.

Frankie stops and looks at me. "Maya! You know what I just figured out? That bird needs a girlfriend and *you* need a girlfriend."

"Oh, Frankie—that's just--! I have a lot of girlfriends!"

But he's right and I am flummoxed that he's seen what I have not: that I've been Franklin's mainstay and he mine, for so many years that I haven't—well, I haven't had the time to get close to anyone

171

else, even the wives of Franklin's business associates, and besides—.

"You could have Miss Peggy or Deano's *mom* for a girlfriend!"

Now it's Sandra's turn to be caught unprepared. Flustered, she assesses me in that microsecond that women use to decide about people, discounts me as a possible buddy, removes her glasses and notices them. "Oh god, were they this dirty in front of Mrs. Stewart?" she moans. "Dean, we must go."

"Must have just happened," I soothe.

Dean heads for the door. "Big Mama needs a lot of food, 'cause she's nursin' all those puppies." He speaks with the authority of a male. Frankie looks pointedly at me and I stoop and pick something up off the floor. I just don't want this talk right now about puppies.

Dean and his mother take their leave, after Dean and Frankie have called each other some good-natured names and punched at each other a few times. Frances and Sandra have said the Required Mothers' Words to each other: "At least they're not old enough yet to date and drive a car!"

The house is quiet again. Frankie has gone outside to ride his bike. All there is for me to do is to put one used glass into the dishwasher. Then sit and watch the Sofa watch me. I'd like to lie down and see if I could nap, but I'm not used to doing that in the daytime. Maybe I just want to get away from people for a while,

172

people who will be after me to get a dog and then to move away, to sell Franklin's books, to forget about him, to tell me I need to have a memorial service, to have the piano tuned, to persuade me that he had a bevy of women he was pursuing-- oh, boy, how could I have been so wrong about Amanda? How could she have been wrong about *me*?

"You look like you've had a long day already, Maya," says Frances, joining me at the kitchen counter. I want to ask her what she has been doing so far, on this one-year occasion. "Mrs. Stewart can be quite the curmudgeon. "

"You weren't scared of her. But she could kill your chances --!" Frances shrugs, starts to say something, plunges in: "Maya, what do you know about taking charge financially of this house?"

"Well, Franklin did it. And you have been taking care of things. It's not as though I have a key to Franklin's desk, you know." That's probably unfair. She and I have never discussed this. She may not know I care. "You know-- for this past year, you have-- I've never given it any thought, actually. I pay the bills that come to me—Macy's, Dillard's, those things. I never see the bills for utilities, electricity--."

"Those are paid online, Maya."

"Really? I didn't know that. And your father gives—gave—you give me an allowance." I don't tell her what I am thinking—that Franklin will take over these tasks himself again when he comes home. He surely wouldn't want me starting this late in the game to be asking him all kinds of questions about his finances.

"Maybe I shouldn't have done it. Maybe I should have let you be in charge of your own house financially. I just took over all the times when he was gone. I needed to keep busy. And as you pointed out, I have the key. I'm sorry if it's a big deal-- let's have a duplicate made. He said it was just to keep Frankie out when he was younger. Don't you think I've been through that room several times, searching for any kind of clue, to make sense of it all?"

"You too?"

"Maya, remember I'm your daughter. I'm not a fool. But you know I took all those business courses, too, so it's only reasonable that it all fell to me."

"Frances. Let's talk about something else."

"No. It's time. You're going to face up to doing this yourself." She laughs. "It's your house, right? And I'll help get you organized. I'll bet you don't even know where the money comes from to pay for everything."

"Well, of course I do!" I answer, stung. People seem to be *crowding* at me so today!

"Dad made it easy for you. It's a slippery slope between respecting another person's wishes and controlling them. Ever think maybe he didn't want you to know what he was doing with all his money?"

174

"No. It's his business."

"Okay. I'm sorry. I'm getting you mad."

"I'm not mad!" I say, mad.

"Okay. Okay. Let me just say this—it looks like he emptied out a bunch of his checking accounts before --before last year."

"You mean we have no money? Then what have we been---?"

"No, no. Don't get upset. It's all right. Apparently he put them all into one bank, because a cashier's check has been coming to you from Boston every month since last June, more than enough to live on. You know the one I give you to endorse? I don't know why he would do things that way, because he never did before and I've been his kind of bill payer for him since Frankie and I moved here."

"But we have enough?"

"*You* have enough. And I'll show you how to do all this because--." She fidgets. "Maya. You know I've been going to church."

I am surprised. Praying for Franklin's return? What a nice thing to do, one which I have done myself countless times.

"And I've been talking with George."

"You've been to see him a lot this past year, I've noticed. Maybe I should have, too. Some counseling, right?" I'm a little irked— Father George should have suggested it for our entire family. Not that I would have necessarily gone, if he was going to change his mind and suggest that Franklin wasn't coming back.

"Well—that, too. And I'm going to have to add some fuel to this terrible anniversary day and I apologize in advance, but I'm going to say what I have to say, anyway." She runs her hands through her sandy-red hair and looks toward the ceiling.

"Oh, Frances—I just don't want to talk about a dog for Frankie again."

"No." She has, I see now, picked up today's mail and has left it on the kitchen counter. She holds the sheaf in her hands and recites as she discards: "Occupant, Occupant, Occupant, Florida Power and Light—it must not be a bill. I pay those online for you. Ad for a new pizza place—"

"Don't throw those Occupant ones away, Frances. I like to see what they are first—"

"—and a letter for me. From a DNA lab."

"Oh, that's a scam. They don't want you to spit into something, do they?"

"No. I already did. These are the results. They just arrived today. There's something quite auspicious to the timing, I think. I haven't looked at them yet. I wanted us to do it together."

My heart spasms. "Oh, Frances. Why did you waste your money on such a foolish thing?"

"One reason only, Maya." She sounds stern. This is so unlike her usual tone of voice that I am alarmed. "Because this is my life and then Frankie's, and not yours. I have to know where I came from. You've been so secretive about it. You used to joke when I was growing up about at least five different states where you might have been born. What's the mystery about? I've seen Dad's birth certificate, but not yours, and I have trouble believing the "building burned down and all the records were lost" story. So. Am I adopted? I can stand knowing. Is my father someone other than Franklin? Are you my real mother?"

"Why—why would you say such a thing? You've seen *your* birth certificate. Do you realize what that says about *me*?"

"Mother—right now today this really is about me, not you."

Suddenly I am afraid I am going faint. I am going to slide right off this barstool and hit my head on the marble tiles. Frances is studying the paper she has taken from its envelope. "Hah! Listen here, Maya—"

I don't want to hear. Particularly on this day. She's going to lose Franklin a second time and I'm not sure I could bear it.

"Frances, please don't—"

"Look! Maya!" She has jumped up from her stool. "It says here that I'm forty-two percent from England—Dad and the Porters-- and forty-nine per cent from Scotland—you, apparently-- McDowell, right?-- and nine percent from northern Africa! Look!

177

Look!" But she's not letting me look. She's waving the paper around. I can make out some kind of colored graph on it.

"That—that can't --no—*Irish*?"

"Because of all this wild red hair? Sorry. Disappointed? I guess we *all* began in Africa, way back. I like that idea." She is re-reading the paper. She is nodding. She has a crooked huge grin on her face. It's the look she had when she showed me Frankie for the first time.

I want to cry in my bafflement. So if this is true, then she is not Red's child. She is Franklin's. All these years, all this hiding, dissembling—and what did it get me? One man dead in a foreign country, dying convinced he had a child by me; one man coming home from a boat that blew up exactly a year ago to a wife and a loving daughter and a bouncy grandson, a man who never doubted for a moment that Frances was his.

But what if this DNA search is wrong? What if it's just a way to get money out of people?

   (*the peregrine rages at me   what if I am not who they say I must be? must I accept being tamed? must I? they have given themselves an impossible task*)

Look at how happy Frances is! Isn't that the point?

My daughter fans herself with the paper. "Now. Whew! Wow. I'm going to need time to process this."

She's back on her stool, her face close to mine. She takes my hand. "Oh! It's like a gift from Dad! I'm so glad it came today!"

She looks ready to dance. "That's just part one, Maya. Part two is that you and I are going to West Virginia—don't give me that look! Yes, we are!-- to see where I came from, after all these years, and you and I are going to do a family history journal together, for Frankie and his kids, if and when he has any."

"Oh, I don't—can't we talk about this later?"

"—and then we're going to Boston to see where all of us Porters came from and we're going to visit the old cemeteries up there."

"And how are we going to pay for these trips?"

"Okay, here's the tough part for you, Maya. *You* are going to acknowledge that Dad is not coming back and *you* are going to sign a paper and *we* are going to get my inheritance and all the money owed us from Dad's estate." She notes my reluctance. "Yes, we *are,* Mother. Yes, we *are.* Or first thing tomorrow Frankie and I pack up and move out of here. And I'm saying this with love, not with any anger."

Pack up and leave? My god! How can she do this to me, today of all days?

"And all this you've discussed with who-- Father George?" I am feeling betrayed. That's twice she has called me "Mother". And Frankie calling me "Grandmother" today! What further control can they take away from me?

179

No, I don't mean that. I don't mean "control". I mean "respect". This has to be entirely Father George's doing. And him bold as brass coming here tonight! What's *his* hidden agenda? A new *pipe organ* as a memorial to Franklin?

"Okay. Let's leave all this aside for now. Let's ask Frankie what we should do-- something fun. I feel like celebrating!"

How had she heard him come in, he was so quiet? Grinning at being discovered, he grabs onto her. "Whatcha want to do now, Frank the Tank?"

"*Not* a movie."

"Okay. What else?"

"Um-m." He's not fooling me, I see. He's already decided. "Bowling!"

"Bowling?"

"Yeah! Deano the Beano and his Mom are going bowling! That's what I want us to do, too!"

"And eat dinner there, at the bowling alley?"

"Yeah! You and me and Maya!" He stops, contrite. "I'm sorry I called you Grandma, Maya."

"I think you were really mad at your teacher, not me, Frankie."

"Yeah!"

He sees he's off the hook. Well, why not? It will keep Frances from asking me more questions, fiddling with my life, at least for a little while. And *I* don't have to bowl, or eat what promises to be wretched food. I'll just sit and watch them and maybe I'll come up with an idea for a poem from the place itself. Actually, that might be a good idea. I just won't bowl. They won't care if I do or not. I'll show them that I'm a good sport, that all those things Frances just said to me have washed right off my back.

I start to hum, "I won't bowl/Don't ask me--."

Frances is showing her son the DNA results. "You and I are partly from Africa? Coo-wull! Wait 'til I tell La'Tischa at school!"

What time is it? Ah, quarter to five. Not much left to this odd day which can't end too soon for me. I feel a little weak-legged and staggery, as though a tornado just swept through the house (well, it did!) and it's all gone now and just feels as though the air has been removed all of a sudden.

I'll talk with Frances tomorrow about signing any papers. I need her to stay with me. Or—maybe I could think about moving into a smaller place. No, that's too much to think about. I need to stay here for when Franklin comes back.

"Frances, do they sell drinks like vodka at the bowling alley?"

Yes, Franklin needs his home to come back to.

181

(come   admire my pinions, my claws, my expression   I know
the plans I have for us   )

Thirteen.

Franklin   10:30 am, 2 days ago   May 15, 2019
Sarasota, Florida

I've always liked this town. I could have disappeared to anywhere on the face of the earth I chose, but for some reason I am quite fond of Sarasota. Can't call it a "town" any more. I used to bring Maya here for theater-going at Asolo, and then to the Ringling Museum and its immense (for Florida) art displays. Maya was always more interested in the size of the kitchen at Ca d'Zan, that palatial mansion built by John Ringling for his beloved wife Mable. "The House of John".

Well, silk purse/pig's ear. At least I tried. Maya always gravitated toward Mable's rose garden. Little interest in the mansion. So I didn't give her a chance when I had our home remodeled. Ca d'Franklin. To coin a Venetian name.

Now, *Peggy,* on the other hand--! What a year we've had here! She's been showing up from Banana Bay just once a month with all the local gossip, leaving me time here to make some private conquests from among the billionaires' bored wives and even better, sometimes their daughters. All the same to me.

While the men are sitting in their private clubs (been there, done that, thank you for my high-toned and classy Boston upbringing, Father and Mother), or lounging on the decks of their oversized yachts that their professional skippers have brought down for them while they themselves arrive in their private jets, to be met at the local airport by pristinely uniformed welcoming chauffeur drivers and limousines (been there, also done that), or they're riding in their golf carts around the oh-so-exclusive golf courses and cheating about their strokes (ditto), I am getting in some good cheating strokes of my own.

This is the city the circus built—the winter resting grounds for the Ringling Brothers/Barnum and Bailey people. How much fun that must have been, those circus roustabouts mixing in with the good ole Sarasota, Florida folks, who must have loved going to be entertained by the high-wire performers trying out their new stunts while the lions roared in their penned areas and the monkeys howled and rattled their cages. Oh, the smell of elephant dung! What days! Two-lane roads, no air conditioning, no advance warning of hurricanes. One hundred sixty acres west of town, out in the countryside back then in 1927 or so.

Then the millionaire money that wanted to spend it in Sarasota in style squeezed all this out. No manure on *their* polished shoes! Followed by tv. When television came in it pretty much finished off the wonderful days of When The Circus Came To Town to those small rural areas, whose citizens could now turn a dial and invite the same kind of entertainment into their living rooms,

184

absent the odor of wild animals and sawdust. And color, of course, at first.

I have to laugh at those rubes newly-arrived to the State of the Shysters buying land in a place outside of Sarasota called Glen Oaks, Glen Pines, always Glen Something; and having pools dug in their ritsy-palatial back yards, only to unearth elephant bones from what was likely Ringling's secret elephant graveyard. Nobody in Sarasota had ever asked where the burial grounds for the aging beasts was; I guess the natives didn't really want to know. I do know that the final pachyderm died in 1956 and nobody asked any questions about his last rites and subsequent earthly resting place.

Now their winter home isn't even in Sarasota. It's been moved up the road to Ellenton, just south of the high-rise bridge into Saint Pete. Guess Sarasota ran out of ivory-tusk memorial gardens.

I feel so at home here that I wonder if I don't have more than a little P.T. Barnum in my blood, except that I wouldn't want to live in Bridgeport, Conn. , home of that loveable "conn" man. I spent a week there one night.

We Americans sure have a soft spot in our hearts for con men like the guys who sold plots of underwater swampland in Florida to the uneducated outsiders. And good old Phineas T. Barnum with his name brand recognition, going around plastering his moniker on every building and fence he came to. Why, he could just as easily have become President if he'd decided to run! (Anyone believe in Reincarnation?)

I'd add my name to the list of frontrunners. President Franklin Porter—has a nice ring to it. But as I've already said about myself, I get bored too fast. Leave that to the latest Man in the White House helping the Rich get Richer. I wish I was still on that list.

I been broke but I never been poor.

All right, enough nostalgia. I am sitting outside in the shade at one of my favorite coffee houses on St. Armand's Circle. European-imported statues of gnomes and dwarves line the circle and the traffic has dwindled since the rich have begun fleeing the upcoming Florida summer for cooler climes. I myself have been housed here almost exactly one year, so I feel a proprietary pleasure in the place.

I have been the most thoughtful guide for Peggy. She had never been to the west coast of Florida. She's not much of a traveler. I took her to Disneyworld once because she insisted. I told her I'd taken Maya there once, so what was the point of going a second time?

But I'll tell you one thing about myself: I am a good sport.

I was bored at Epcot until I decided to play the game Mother and I used to play, to amuse ourselves while we waited in one hotel lobby or another for Father to finish with his business up in some skyscraper board room.

I was just getting myself warmed up in the sport of it here amongst the Common People wearing round felt ears on their beanies, smiling to myself the way winners in life do when we are handed ribbons, medals, loving cups, and rather yearning for Mother and her infectious laugh—god, sometimes after all these years I still miss those times!-- when Peggy found me in the crowd. She'd been on one more of those rides where you have to be This Tall, patiently tolerating the heat and the pushing, the crowding. The crowding is that which gives me an advantage, actually.

"Hey! What the hell are you doing, Franklin?"

"Oh. You mean this?" I looked up from the trash can where I had been oh-so-surreptitiously discarding emptied wallets and the like. "Just passing time waiting for you, my lovely."

She frowned. "You know that's wrong, don't you?"

I shrugged. Unlike Mother, Peggy could be a real drag on my good cheer. "Come on. Hey, how was your ride? Me, I've had enough of this place. Let's go drink ourselves silly and find a room in a fancy hotel that doesn't allow children."

"*You're* a child, Franklin." The way she looked at me and then spun away so fast she bumped into an old geezer driving an electric cart, for a moment I wondered if she was going to turn me in. But then she apologized to him-- for what, I wondered, he was in *her* way. Everybody's always in somebody else's way. That thought made me laugh out loud! Yes, indeedy, the happiest place on earth! Well, then she came back to me (they always do) and we carried on as though she had not had this wearisome touch of Puritan ethics, which fortunately had passed me by on its way to the Wall Street era.

Peggy seemed to like simple entertainment, so in Sarasota I took her on the Mangrove Tunnel tour, to Haunted Sarasota, even to the Circus behind the mall, which turned out to be a big top over a stripped-down one-ring remnant of Ringling with dog, horse, acrobatic routines—and crowds of gawkers for me to practice my skills on.

Now I glance absent-mindedly at the tourists milling on the sidewalks around the Circle. Easter was later than usual this year—April twenty-first—so college kids and teenagers on school breaks have been overrunning this quaint roundabout area across the causeway, just west of Sarasota proper and just east of the Gulf, with so much noise, chaos and drinking that you would think they were all rock concert-amplifier deaf—which, maybe they are.

Lots of car horns. These kids are looking down all the time. What is so damned urgent that they would step out blindly into the street while staring at their cellphones? If one should want to leave them flailing like fish left flopping on the beach after a wave drops them there and recedes, a way to do it would be to take their cell phones away. I can just picture their indignant faces.

Ah, Franklin, Franklin, I'm afraid you're sounding rather cranky and old today. Point is, I've had to have my eyes tested since I've moved here and it has been advised that I need *bifocals,* of all things.

And a couple of crowns.

I'm also swilling antacids on a regular basis. Not happy about this. I've believed that time doesn't stand still, but I always thought it pertained to other people, not me.

I haven't swum in a while, although I have been getting out almost daily to the Gulf off Longboat Key, where I have rented rather an artist's studio—surprisingly charming, although sparse. I escape its drift-woody walls often to drive this way south to St. Armand's.

I even look like an artist. I have dyed my hair and grown a beard. I would be hard to recognize, even by any of my father's old Boston banker types, should they chance upon me. I was a little irritated to discover so much gray in my beard, so have been dyeing that in private and I think it looks quite sporty. Carefully selected wealthy women have told me so.

I am wearing the newly young-moneyed area's "costume"—faded designer label blue jeans; expensive leather belt with a chunky BMW buckle that I was quick enough to spot at a thrift store, of all places; a long-sleeved white expensive shirt of a material that only the in-the-know riche would recognize, not those sales-seekers from Sears Outlet World; open at the neck (the silk cravat having been put away for the summer); sleeves rolled up to reveal the Rolex watch; deck shoes with no socks; dark glasses. No wedding band. (I note that the pale line on my fourth finger, left hand with the ring removed has joined my tan in the Florida sun).

You can tell local people from the tourists—only the tourists wear tee shirts advertising anything, funny or otherwise. There are some aging white big-bellied sunburnt geezers here and there wearing those damned red MAGA caps, but otherwise, the place looks pretty apolitical.

I've been through most of the shops here on the Circle. I've seen some outstanding plays (again, for Florida—please do not remind me what a snob I am) at Asolo. I've taken yet another tour through their original theater, brought here from Italy—Asolo people call it their "jewel box". Sadly, there are only a few of the original professional actors on stage from when Maya and I first began coming here. Now they're all kids. Even Lear wore a white wig and painted facial lines, quite vivid to me when I saw the play by myself as I sat up close to the footlights. I do things that amuse only me, like play attending, when Peggy's not here.

190

I signal for a refill of my coffee and I slump a little in my chair underneath the restaurant's awning. The sun is not yet high, so the air has not warmed to being uncomfortable yet today, but there's sunshine creeping onto my table now. I may have to move. There's canned music coming from somewhere. As the cars go by I can hear snatches of Taylor Swift (Peggy has been educating me) or talk radio (please do not attempt to "educate" me). Yapping dogs remind me momentarily of a debt I owe Frankie as a grandfather. I set that thought aside.

I look up as a couple of women walk by, chatting away, assessing me as boldly as I mark them. What has happened to the demure other sex? Now they wear shorts going up into their crotches, and skin-tight tops. Their breasts ride high and full like the prow of a ship. Their makeup jobs are impeccable and their legs tanned and smooth. Their hair flows behind. Their ages? Who can tell anymore? Nowadays everyone to me looks embalmed while still breathing—artificiality abounds. They might even be male. Who can tell?

Perhaps you can ascertain that I'm a—well, let's just say, a wee bit—morose today. My money, taken from my bank accounts in Banana Bay after I did all that research about how to live off the grid, is diminishing at a faster rate than I would have dreamed possible.

Well, seasonal rates here in Sarasota. . . and one still needs AC. And a serviceable vehicle.

Peggy has been with me this time for an entire week. I find that a week with her (with any woman, actually) becomes rather tedious. (How did I stand all those years with Maya, except by leaving so often?) Peggy seemed a little miffed that I wanted to skimp on the restaurants I took her to, telling her we could split a meal, walk on the beach instead of going to a nightclub show, see a matinee film, things like that. I've paid her plenty—that condo of hers was no chump change-- to keep quiet about where I am, but I never thought money would come between us.

That's a joke. Money comes between everyone, sooner or later.

So this morning, just a couple of hours ago, I woke up to catch her packing her suitcase and trying to be quiet about it, but not succeeding. She watched me sit up in bed, but she didn't stop.

"Franklin. This just isn't working."

"Sure it is," I mumbled. My mouth felt fuzzy from last night's drinking. Damned well drinks.

"No. I'm living two lives. I'm back in Banana Bay, where I run into people I know who know—who knew you. It's getting harder for me to keep my story straight. My friend Amanda wants to know where I keep disappearing to."

"Oh, come on, that's easy— a sick aunt. "

"No, I really mean it this time."

And then I spotted with disbelief what she had just dropped into her suitcase.

"Hey! Wait a minute, Peggy! Dammit!—that book's not yours!" She gave me a sour look and kept packing.

 My book! It's a first edition of "Huckleberry Finn". I found it— under, of all things, the bookstore's cat, which was stretched out on it, as asleep as a cat ever lets itself get. Peggy and I love that bookstore, in an old building in downtown Sarasota, three stories of who knows what—memorabilia and literary gems mixed together with Mickey Spillanes. The Mark Twain, once I blew the Persian hair off it and asked the price, was more than I had been ready to pay; and buying it gave me a huge twinge when I thought of all the books I had left behind in Maya's clumsy hands, but I *had* to have it.

And how dared Peggy act as though it was hers!

I couldn't grab it out of her suitcase without her giving me a fight and possibly harming it. Besides, my bladder was full to overflowing and I feared she was waiting for the moment I headed to the bathroom, to bolt and leave me in a very vulnerable position.

So I acted on impulse.

I hit her in the eye with my fist.

When she reeled back in pain, giving a yelp, I grabbed up the book, high-tailed it into the bathroom, shut and locked the door, and in my haste—dropped "Huckleberry Finn" into the open toilet.

(Here I must take responsibility. Peggy, and before her, Maya, had been after me to keep the lid down. I, seeing no sense in that, and judging what a waste of time it was having to put the lid up each time I wanted to take a piss, had fought both women with different toilets, in passive-aggressive style over it. *A man's gotta take a stand!* was my joke at the time.)

In horror, visions of Huck on a raft in the river danced in front of my eyes. I fished the now semi-useless novel from the bowl. I still had an intense need to urinate, so the book had to wait dripping, the pages swelling atop the undersized towel I used as a bathmat, while I performed my bodily function.

In the midst of this I heard the door slam. Helpless (how could I have *stored* all this fluid?) I was forced to let her go without even a chance to survey the damage I had done to her poor face and to properly apologize.

So instead, I dried off the book as well as I could. I swore at myself over and over again, but what good did that do? She had even taken her hair dryer, so I would never know if that would have worked on the soggy pages.

Okay. Now I needed something to eat, but there was no food in the tiny kitchenette except a sad-looking jar of Peggy's favorite pickles (after all I did for that woman! I lamented) from Ye Olde

Gourmet Shoppe. So I headed for St. Armand's Circle, to join the unwashed herds who would not have known Samuel Clemens from any other snowy-haired gentleman dressed completely in white—idiots!

You think my day could not go worse? Hah. Some woman's pocketbook-sized dog tried to hump my leg. What was most likely a Killer bee came out of nowhere and circled me while I batted it away with a menu showing foodstuffs that I was now hard-pressed to afford, and looking to passersby as though I was doing some weird kind of fan dance. A totally gorgeous young woman (could have been a male actor in drag—I know I need bifocals) crossing the street right in front of my table looked up from her cellphone and actually sniggered. And while I have been pondering the supreme unfairness of my life, my coffee has grown cold.

All at once, as though reading my mind, a man's shadow falls across my table. A waiter. Good. "More coffee, please," I say. "Regular, not decaf."

"Franklin," the man says.

I look up.

And I swear to you that unless global warming causes the world to end this very minute, nothing else can surprise me. Well, sure, if Rocco were to materialize and stick a gun into my ribs--.

"Hello, Father."

*　　　　*　　　　　*

Well, I of course have to ask him to sit down. Maybe at the least he'll pay for my brunch. "What are you doing here?"

What an inane question. God, he looks old. I wouldn't have recognized him, except that no one ever said my two-syllable name the way he just did. How many years since I've seen him? Thirty-four years since I had spoken with him on the phone long distance while I told him I was marrying Maya and he had disinherited me. Thank God for Mother's money! Twenty-six when I was born. So that makes him—

The man sits patiently, breathing in a labored way while I muster my headachy brain to do some math, and he reads my mind, the same way he used to do when I was young. "I am now eight-four years old, Franklin." He signals to the waiter. Ah—the convicted man gets a last meal. I'd better make it a good one.

We both order cracked crab cocktails and the fish (something imported from halfway around the world, although we are but a mile from fresh catches) of the day. I order a double martini and more coffee.

"I cannot drink anymore," my father intones. "Or smoke a cigar. I have come simply to fetch you and to take you home."

196

"B--Boston?" I ask, confused.

"Banana Bay. I have decided I must become acquainted on a personal basis, face to face, with my daughter-in-law, my granddaughter and great-grandson before I die." He taps impatiently on the red Spanish-tiled floor with what looks like a most expensive cane.

"How did you know I have--?" Stupid question. He found *me*, didn't he?

But I won't give in to him all that easily. "Sorry, no. I'm not going back. I prefer it here." He arouses my stubbornness. I dare not look like a failure in front of him, even though I am going to let him pick up the check. I'm actually playing for time. He and Peggy have both given me enough starts this morning for a genuine heart attack.

"Franklin, think. How did I find you?"

"All right—how?"

"It's not all that difficult to trace a person. I did it through the parcels of cash you were sending a Peggy Something."

"You took advantage of our United States Post Office? That—that has to be illegal!" I sputter.

"Franklin, Franklin. You know we live by different rules than ordinary people."

I concentrate on my crab cocktail, which I mourn that I can no longer afford on my own.

My father is continuing: "I've had you traced and followed for the better part of a year. Well, off and on for years before that, but we won't go into it at this time. I have never believed in indolence and I kept hoping you were making a fresh start. But really, Franklin. That wild tale about drowning. . . !"

I laugh. "You're making that up, Father. Traced? Impossible. I would have noticed, surely." Yet a part of my brain shrinks away from the idea that if he could find me, then possibly Rocco could, too.

My father does not reply. Instead he nods at a nearby table where a tall black man with a clean-shaven head, his lean frame impeccably suited in this heat and wearing dark sunglasses, the kind where you can't see the wearer's eyes at all, nods impassively back. See, now that is just the sort of con *I* would do if I wanted to convince someone I was following him—gesture to a stranger like that.

I must have made a face, because my father says, "Have you seen my man Dexter at all? Anywhere? At Publix? At Ringling? At that bookstore you frequent? At the front desk where you are living?"

Dexter. What a made-up name. I snort. "No, of course not!"

My father nods approvingly. "That's how good he is and how he's worth the money I pay him." He pushes his mostly-eaten cocktail away. I am hungry enough that I am tempted to say, "Hand it over to me." A waiter appears.

"Everything all right, Mr. Porter?"

"Yes, thank you, Reggie."

I've been here all year and I've never learned Reggie's name! My father smiles at me as though we share a secret. "Money talks, my son. You know that. And your money right now is pretty nigh unto giving its last dying gasps. Don't sulk. I know that look."

"I need to think about this, that's all. You've really hit me hard, surprising me, coming at me--I mean, you show up here out of nowhere--!"

"You and I both know that Boston is not nowhere. *Banana Bay* is nowhere."

"—and—and then you tell me some crazy story about how a guy with a totally made-up name like Dexter has been—!"

"Franklin, stop. I told you that I'm close to dying. How much time do you think I'm going to give you to consider what I'm telling you?" He taps his cane. "I swear you get your quirky way of thinking from your mother." He smiles. "Still keeping her china?"

I react. "Okay. You got me."

"Certainly I 'got you'. So did she. She swore to you that it was priceless, didn't she?"

I am stunned. "No?" My own *mother* cheated me? "No!"

"No. Let me tell you something, Franklin—you take two born excitement seekers like your mother and me and you put them together, and they have such fun fooling each other all the time that it's like a game to them-- and to me, to find a woman like that with such an inborn sense of deception, and who loves *using* it— well, I tell you, son—the times we had! When we were young, of course."

I am taking this extremely personally, I realize. He's talking about my mother, for god's sake!

"No, no, she really did have all those headaches and she really was not able to have any more children after you. Now that I think of it, maybe she could have. Maybe she did something about it when you were born. I wouldn't have put it past her to give her doctor some cock-and bull-story about some dread disease in her family and get him to feeling oh-so-lucky that she had had herself a healthy one here, and better not take any more chances. We put all our eggs in your basket, to make light of it. And she was good to you and she loved you as much as a—what's the word these days?—as much as a charming, brilliant sociopath could. She never dangled you off a bridge for sport, as far as I know, or left you neglected out in the rain. No, she took good enough care of you. Well, all right—she did her share of *lying* to you, but it was just more of a romp to her, you see."

"And I suppose you considered yourself so—so upright!"

"Someone in the family had to make the money."

"So—are you calling her—amoral?"

"Tut tut, Franklin." I can't believe people actually say, "Tut tut" any more.

I persist. "Then-- am I yours? Your biological son?" I am suddenly wrestling with an interesting dilemma, which I would love to have more time to peruse—did I inherit my zest for life from my mother or merely learn it from her?

 I had recently skimmed a book at the Sarasota bookstore (musing over whether or not I should pocket it while the cat looked on, preening herself) about how every twenty-fourth person born is a sociopath, which would make it four out of every hundred. I didn't care for those odds. I like to think of myself as much more extraordinary than that. And I wouldn't label either Mother or me that, either. Still, I had some curiosity about reading more.

So I pocketed the book. I started reading it, but as I said, I get bored easily. So into the trash it went. That's a laugh—Huck Finn into the crapper and this stupid book primed to be recycled.

"As far as I can tell. Franklin, you listening? Your mother's folks came from up near Loch Ness and mine came from places around

London, although that was centuries ago. I truly believe you look like me, like a Porter. Not in hair color, of course, because your mother loved changing hers all the time--." He laughs. "Franklin, do you remember that time she dyed it bright green for St. Patrick's Day?"

I have to turn the knife just one more time. "Yes, well—I don't think my daughter is biologically mine."

"Are you sterile, Franklin? That would make my search for an heir a dead end."

Wow. That one hurts more than the zinger I just gave him! But all those women I had over all those years, and nobody—not even Peggy—not the least, not even when I was careless or in a hurry-- *huh.*

"Father, I've never said this, not even to Maya, but—I guessed she was pregnant when I met her. She was too willing to throw herself at me. I think I was the means to get her out of Jerome. Oh, I don't blame her. Not anymore. *I* couldn't stand the place, either." I say this although I hardly remember it now.

"Franklin, you must stop dilly-dallying. I have no other son. Of this I am certain. I have no other offspring. As far as I am concerned, my granddaughter and great-grandson are legally mine. Don't you go mucking up the works now."

"Damn. It's just--I just thought my money would last longer than it has."

"That's always the case. Let me ask you--have you done anything illegal in Banana Bay?"

"Uh—no. Not that I know of." (Technically, my dealings with Rocco were in Cocoa, not Banana Bay.)

"You can go back there and not be arrested?"

"As far as I know."

"Going to use the amnesia trick?"

"It won't work. It won't explain away the money I withdrew before I 'drowned' at sea."

"That's a pity. Well, you may face some jail time and some healthy fines. The Coast Guard doesn't like to be made fools of, nor do the banks and the police departments." He pauses. "You're a healthy strapping boy. You'll survive."

He looks at me, a long almost loving look. "I'll help see you through this, financially and any other way I can, as long as I'm around." He hesitates and looks at me almost sheepishly. Is he going to confess to a crime also? That would certainly put us on more equal footing. I prepare not to be surprised.

"Franklin--I am deeply disappointed in you in one financial area: that of caring for your family."

"I cared for them!"

"I've been keeping track. They would have run out of wherewithal rather rapidly if I had not stepped in with monthly checks of my own for them."

(I have to confess that once I was in the car with Peggy that dark night after I had had my all-too-invigorating swim, it was for Maya out of sight, out of mind.)

"Why, Father—that's most generous of you!" I can tell he doesn't buy my empty compliment. "Father, this will sound trite, but-- I'm sincerely sorry I caused you such trouble when I was younger."

"I never did disinherit you, you know. Such a bother to do that. So you owe me, son."

"You've gotten quite crafty in your dotage, Sir."

"I have always been crafty, Franklin."

We look at each other and this is where we came the closest to hugging one another; but I think if we had, we would have started sobbing, the two of us who had once been so close and so entertained (although, come to think of it, no one else had been) by Mother's shenanigans—a string of parking tickets here, a shoplifted mink coat there-- and who had found each other again after all these decades.

However, we did not hug, not we Porter men, standing now side to side, looking so much alike except for our age differences, waiting while one of us paid the bill and the other looked for a sleight-of-hand way to edge the tip money off the table and into the jeans pocket; we two Porters who could trace our lineage all the way back to the Constitution, who would not be so common as to weep, even when amongst strangers in Sarasota whom we would (the good Lord be merciful) never meet again.

Fourteen.

Franklin   May 16-17, 2019   from Sarasota to Banana Bay

Father and I did not return home to Banana Bay that afternoon, for quite a mundane reason: there had been something off about the cracked crab cocktail. Father very kindly and most hurriedly procured for me another suite adjoining his at the Radisson on the Gulf, where each suite had two beds, but only one bath (one bath not sufficing for the two of us in our immediate critical conditions). So we spent most of our times in our respective bathrooms with only a wall between us and our shared misery, puking our brains out and then resting fitfully.

I was surprisingly concerned about him because of his age and his physical condition, but he seemed to come through the whole ordeal as well as I did. (Huck Finn in the morning and now this in the afternoon, I thought miserably to myself at one point as I cooled my forehead against the floor tile. From one bowl to another. My life.)

We left the sliding glass doors to the balconies wide open to dissipate the odor. Father paid the maids handsomely to keep returning to our wretched (a feeble joke, we were both so feeble) porcelain thrones for cleanings.

That was on the first day, in the afternoon and evening. By the second day all we wanted to do was sip ginger ale and chicken broth and eat crackers, brought to us by the shaved-headed Dexter, for whom the phrase "tall, dark and handsome" seemed to have been written; who turned out to be in truth Father's Man and our mute guardian angel. I never heard Dexter open his mouth to speak. I imagined in my misery that Father had rescued him from some horrendous foreign prison, where Dexter had had his tongue cut out during torture.

What facilities Father's Dexter used, where he slept, where he ate, how he knew intuitively when he was needed, I was not aware of. I would have thought to ask him, but to what avail? It was obvious the man could not speak and I refused to add to his burden of woe by interrogating him, nor was I that interested, truth be told. And so, spent, our alimentary tracts at last empty, we collapsed on the beds in Father's suite. We slept a lot, whiling away our time together thus.

I asked, the first afternoon of the worst cramps, lying between Father's beds, the phone to my ear on the floor, and actually panting like a dog in the Banana Bay August heat, that a doctor be sent to our rooms. I was too wasted to demand anything (my usual method of communicating with those other than my equals); but eventually (I credit Dexter) a medico appeared, pronounced us both to be suffering from slight cases of food poisoning (there is nothing slight to a 'slight case', I can assure you), gave us prescriptions for anti-nausea medications, which Dexter dutifully and silently took to be filled for us. This same physician sent Father an inflated bill for making a house call, which Father thought quite reasonable and which convinced me that I had been pinching pennies for so long now that I had lost my perspective.

"We should sue the restaurant!" I croaked in a hoarse voice to the doctor, "How do we go about doing that? How many more cases of this are you seeing?"

"Or," the doctor said, seeing his way out and having to live here with the restaurant owners after we were long gone, "you two might just have a case of the twenty-four hour bug."

So went a way for us (read "me", always the opportunist) to make some easy money.

I must repeat that Father's Man Dexter, having eschewed the cracked crab, was like our guardian angel. Of course, knowing Father, I assumed he was being paid handsomely, but even so, he drove up to my artist's hideaway and packed my few belongings, even the Huckleberry Finn, which I was too wracked and wrecked to even care about while I was lying on the bathroom floor. My guess is that he had once been a government agent—Father told me Dexter swept the room thoroughly for any traces of me—just in case. In case of what, I did not ask.

When at last Father and I could rest on the beds in the same room, we talked about making plans, about how difficult it might be for me to walk abruptly back into Maya's life (I had not considered that), let along that of Banana Bay. I didn't bring up her name, but figured that I'd probably not be allowed to see Peggy ever again and for that I was sorry. I really owed her an apology. So unlike me to apologize for anything. It must have been the medication talking.

So like God, but on the second day, we rested. That meant that it would put us back at my house on the seventeenth of May, a day I saw as comically auspicious, since it would be precisely one year to the day when I had bobbed in the ocean and talked to the porpoises.

"Tell me what you are driving, Franklin." That was my father, all business. I was sure he was testing me, sure that Dexter had already uncovered this information.

"Uh—a 2019 Ferrari. Silver. It's leased." I gave him the license plate number. "It may have been towed by now, though."

"A Ferrari," my father scoffed as well as he could from a supine position, "and you in the garb of a starving artist." Before I could take offense to my well-thought-out wardrobe he flicked a finger toward his Man. "Dexter."

The Man nodded. "Dexter, you know what to do."

Dexter nodded again and left the room. I had a spurt of something like sadness, realizing that I would never hear what Dexter's voice had once sounded like. Those damned Commies in those damned foreign countries! My father turned his head toward me, the younger supine Porter, and gave me a look which I realized I had missed most of this last year: that's what money can do.

"Uh, Father—if you asked Dexter to, uh—calm down a guy named Rocco, do you think--?"

"Already done. Safe to go home." And with this kind of breezy everyday discourse, we whiled away the afternoon and evening of the day before our departure.

"I'm turning over a new leaf, Father. . . No, I really mean it this time. . . I'm not getting any younger. . . . Did I tell you I'm going to need two crowns? Father?"

His eyes were shut. I studied him, this man who had rescued me so many times and appeared willing to keep on doing it. His hair, and there was still a lot left of it, which gave me hope,

was white and his pallor rather pale, even for a New Englander. I noted the indentations on both sides of his nose where his glasses usually rested. Stretched out, he was as tall as I, although when we stood he was more bent over. I guessed that the cane was necessary. Still, if I had to compare him to other men his age, he was quite a handsome devil. Both my parents had been generous in the passing on of good-looking genes.

I heard him snore and soon I too drifted off, with visions of prime rib and champagne dancing in my head, Santa Claus a tall, dark, bald and silent gift-bringer.

Fifteen.

Maya   5:30 pm   May 17, 2019   Banana Bay Bonanza Bowling Lanes

<u>Lone Ranger</u>   a poem by Maya Porter   2010

This is the fifth Tonto who's left me.

He got mad when I told him

We can't take a vacation

'cause I have to save money

To buy silver bullets.

Huh.   S'pose he thinks it's easy

Keepin' lookout fer bad guys

Aidin' the underdogs

Gallopin' off 'fore

They gets to thank me.   Now

What if, jest once, I was to

Hang around afterwards

Yank off my face mask

Drink likker with all of 'em?

Nah.   They'd say,

"Hey, look, I know him!

He's Miz Tucker's kid!"—

"Well, whaddya know!

Miz Tucker's kid helped us?

That little squirt, the one never would smile?"

Then they'd all howl.   Nah.

Better to stay like this

Masked up and helpful

Even if it could mean

Goin' through Tontos.

Nobody understands

My mission anyhow.

It's lonely waitin'

It's tough bein' vigilant

It's rough never relaxin'

But it sure beats bein' laughed at.   And

My Ma would approve.

                *   *   *

I'm only going to sit and watch, I told myself. Just sit and watch. Maybe read.

What a joke on me—I have neglected to bring a book along; the bowling alley's lighting does not lend itself to reading; and the noise level is worse than that of a church service with all the organ stops out and everyone singing "Lift high the Cross!" at top volume.

Frankie and Dean are ecstatic at being here. I look at the size of the bowling balls and wonder how they will manage.

"Don't worry," Frances shouts into my ear. "There are a couple of special lanes just for kids, with lighter-sized balls. They get to start halfway up the alley toward the pins. Here, I got you a pair of shoes too, in case you change your mind. "

So I, like a good sport, try on the shoes. "They're a size seven. They're brand-new. Look. No one has ever worn them. Great, right, Maya?"

"Great." My daughter is aware that I don't like wearing anyone's shoes except my own, the way I had to wear hand-me-downs as a child, although she doesn't know the reason. I try on the bowling shoes, which do fit, even though they are a little stiff.

(I wish now, trying to re-create the next thirty minutes, that I had checked the bottom of those shoes.)

The boys are already playing in their special lane next to us. The noise level seems to have risen to that of the roar of Niagara Falls. Up close.

"So!" Sandra stands over us as Frances and I lace up. "Ready to play?"

Now I had only played once when I was a young mother, but they are young mothers too, so—sure. "Sure, I'll play. Why not?"

"Great!" Sandra has brought with her three other young women and they all look—vigorous. As though they work out all the time. They add their several children to the lane with the boys, everyone talking at the same time. I haven't seen this amount of cheeriness since we volunteers counted the profits after St. Swithins' annual rummage sale last month.

It is so noisy here, what with pins being knocked down all over the place and the balls cannoning down the alleys and the bang-

clank of balls being returned to their starting positions, that I'm
under the impression that Sandra's three friends have all been
introduced to me as Tracey.

"Where's Tracey?" asks Frances.

Really? Just look around, I think.

"She couldn't make it," says Sandra, weighing a bowling ball and
choosing another.

"Then we'll need to take turns. We have an odd number. Unless
someone wants to just sit."

"Oh. Your mother decided not to play?" Sandra looks at me. I
realize it is a look of "you scatterbrained matron who misplaces
innocent children," so I smile a big smile and say, "Of course I'm
playing!"

I scan the different bowling balls as carefully as I can without
drawing any attention to myself. It's been so many years, but--. It
looks as though their weights are stamped on them, so I look for
the lowest number. And then there's the question of holes—I
notice that balls might have the same weight number, but different
sized holes for the digits. I am so glad I didn't ask Mr. Lu to do
my fingernails. And the balls are different colors, too—might that
be a symbol for something?

In the end and because the kids keep screaming and jumping up
and down and when they do, their mothers jump up and down in
encouragement, although lord knows those kids don't need any

more adrenalin pumped into them than is already there, I feel the pressure to decide.

The pushy peregrine inside me is silent. Smart bird.

And the kids haven't even started filling up on the carb-heavy foods that I bet are the only items served here. At least it's Friday. No school tomorrow. They can get as doped up as they want and then sleep it off.

"Ready?" Frances calls to me. I smile and wave at her and then pick a random bowling ball just because the color is less garish than the others and matches my toenail polish, although at this juncture my toes are covered. Ocean Wattah.

"Come on! Your turn!" The other Traceys all motion me. "Your turn!"

I hold the ball with two fingers and the thumb of my left hand. This is my dominant hand, the one I write with, and I pray it is the correct one to use. I cup the ball underneath with my right hand, the way I just watched someone else do it.

"It's easy!" Frances urges me. "Count your steps! One-two-three and throw the ball. Right down the center. Just keep it out of the gutter."

Well, that seems simple enough. So I step up to the alley, count one-two-three steps and let go the ball, which wobbles its way down to the pins, staying out of the gutter and magically in a kind of slow motion knocking seven of them down as I stand there staring at what I have done.

"Seven, seven, lucky seven!" Frances yells. One of the Traceys appears behind me. "My turn," she says.

Oh. I need to get out of the way now. She throws her ball in a clean kind of arc and knocks down—four pins.

I beat her! I beat her! Maybe I am a natural at this! Well, I can show these younger women that there's a helluva lot of piss and vinegar in me yet! No friends, my ass! They're *all* going to want to be my friends!

This is a huge bowling alley. TV screens up and down, over where the pins are set up, show how many pins there are left and every now and then show the bowlers. There must be at least 15 lanes here, seemingly stretched end to end to infinity. This is a world I had never thought about (nay, cared about if I am to be honest) until this afternoon.

And there's Frances, in beautiful form! I know, because one of the Traceys says, "I sure admire her form."

"Great form, Frances! Great form!" I yell. Down at the far end of the bowling alley a bunch of people are waving our way frantically, but since I am not wearing my glasses I have no idea who they are waving at. I wave back anyway.

"You're up again, Maya," a Tracey says. Already? Okay. Just let me find my ball.

Going by color and then by number I locate the ball. Now. All I have to do is count.

"One. Two. Three."

I swing the ball. That's the easy part. To my astonishment there is suddenly an urgent double situation: my new bowling shoes—uh-h!-- adhere themselves like Indy Five Hundred brake pads to the floor; and the bowling ball won't let go my fingers.

I am down BAM! before I have time to realize what is happening. There is a moment of non-reaction as the Traceys and Frances (she tells me at home afterward) absorb with disbelief the picture of me, lying there with my face in the gutter, while I attempt to assess my condition.

Agh! A-AGH-H! Here's a sickly pain I remember vividly: I am fourteen. I slip on a wet rock at Jerome High and my left hand goes down to break my fall. I feel something snap in that hand, my poem-writing hand. The back of it starts to swell.

My Momma refuses to think anything is wrong with me and she sticks my hand in some hot dishwater while I scream in pain. She gives me an aspirin and by the next morning my hand is really swollen and useless. I pant as I use toilet paper in the bathroom, forcing me to switch to my seldom-used right hand and confusing my brain which is already shooting me sickly pain signals.

Momma still refuses to take me to a doctor—I know it's the money part that bothers her-- so I, in an assertive act that causes me to catch my breath even after all those years, say to her, "All right. If you won't take me to the doctor, I'll get one of our neighbors to do it."

Hot with West Virginia pride, she takes me to the doctor's, where an x-ray verifies a broken bone. I stride from his office into the waiting room, my left hand and lower arm held high in its new pristine-white plaster cast, and I shout a teenager's sarcastic shout so that my Momma and the entire room of people sitting there can take notice, "See? *I told you so!*"

This is the same pain. The body and the brain remember. They have no sense of time.

"Get up, Maya," I hear Frances say. "Come on, get up." She sounds like the stag in the Disney cartoon, the one where the fire scared me so badly. "Maya!"

I cannot.

Then there is a woman's familiar husky voice in my ear. "Think you broke somethin'?" I am helped up to a sitting position. My head is swimming. "What hurts? No, Maya! Don't you pass out now. Hey! Somebody! Get a cold towel over here! Stat! *Now!*" To me the person says, "Put your head down. We don't want you passin' out."

"Maya? Whoa! What happened?" I hear Frankie's voice, much more excited than worried, and then that of Frances: "I don't understand. One minute she was up and the next she was down flat--!"

"My shoes stuck," I mutter, my head down around my knees.

"Show me where it hurts," says the voice next to my ear and I gingerly raise my left arm. I wiggle my fingers to be sure I didn't leave any in the bowling ball. Now my—YOW!—right one.

"I'm runnin' my fingers gently up your arm. Tell me when it hurts." When she comes to the upper right arm I almost pass out. "Right humerus. Okay. Maya—we needa git you to the emergency room for x-rays."

"Already I called. Told them on way," a man's deep voice announces.

The pain is making me feel nauseated, but now I recognize the woman's voice. I glance up sideways, carefully—Brenda! Brenda from my "Poor Me" class! "What-what the hell are you doing here?"

"Hey, Maya. You sure fell on a good night. The church bowlin' league is here."

"But how do you know which bone--?" I gasp, the pain announcing itself.

"I'm a paramedic. Hey! Listen up! Who's takin' Miss Maya to the hospital?"

"I take," booms that deep now-familiar voice. "I take Miss Maya."

This day has just become even weirder. "Max." I must be hallucinating.

A couple of men have entered with a stretcher. "I go, you stay," Max is telling someone. "You take your kid, I take your mother. He eats. Let him finish. You find us at hospital. Hah. Stand back. I got." So Max is the one who is lifting me up, being so careful of my right arm, while I scream in pain at the slightest movement.

There's an instant sight of Frankie's face, excited, next to mine. "You're an oofie," I tell him. Then I'm on the stretcher. I hear Max introducing himself to Frances. "Hey! Don't you faint, too," Brenda is saying to someone, possibly my daughter. Maybe one of the Traceys.

I feel a pinprick and then relief. I must have been given a shot. "Just for the pain and the nausea," someone says. "We can't let her go to sleep, in case she hit her head."

"I felt her head," I hear Brenda say. "No sign of concussion. She was lucky—she coulda broke her nose. Funny thing that I was comin' over here that very second to say hi. Bam! She went right over like a dead tree gettin' cut down!"

"God *told* you to come over here!" one of the Traceys says in a prayerlike voice, or maybe someone in the church bowling league. It's not something Episcopalians would say.

Maybe I could write a poem about this:

"Oh, I hope they have movies in heaven

Just picture me there on a cloud

Where the films that make me cry

Reach up past the sky

And there's not a single bowling ball allowed."

Oh! That's good! I need a pencil. . . .

"Somebody take off my red shoes," I murmur, the way Moira Shearer did in that 1940s movie after she did the ballet leap in front of a moving train. I am determined that I will not go to the hospital in these clunkers. I have great-looking toenails and I want them to show. I am one half of Banana Bay's Beautiful Couple. Just not in bowling shoes.

Sixteen.

Maya   **8:15 pm**   **May 17, 2019**

At home

Lines From Imperfect Motherhood   a poem by Maya Porter

2017

I have heard it said

The healthiest people have no bearing of grievances

To keep them awake. Why then must I be bound by my

Catechismic-like beads, my list of past sins

Spooling off in the dark:

The time I would not let her

 Wear her favorite miniskirt to church.

(I thought I was right)

The time I saw her off to camp.

She asked for a restroom first. I told her

(I thought I was right)

There was one on the bus. Now decades later

Her young trusting face shines up at me, and I wince. Stop.

I need instead to remember: always her shoes fit;

Always for her a meal, always for her a clean-sheeted bed. Surely

These counted! These were ideals! And yet (how small, to be right)

Perhaps they were not.

*   *   *

Paramedic Brenda was correct—my right humerus was broken, although the good news from the x-ray showed that I wouldn't need surgery. The fractured bone would heal itself.

After the pain reliever kicked in, Max and I had nothing to do except to wait. I had stopped gasping as the medication took hold, so we just sat. I had not talked at length to another man (or woman) in a year. Talking to Franklin usually meant trying to catch up with him and then grab onto his overcharged, short attention span. So Max did most of the talking at first. We talked and then just sat; and then sat and talked some more.

I told him about my poems. He told me he would "admire" to read them. He told me about his love of art. He recited a few short poems to me, too, in his native language. I couldn't think of even one of mine to recite back to him.

He told me his sister Elena loves my class and that she was out tonight with Kathy, who had taken Elena home with her to spend the night. They were planning to stay in Kathy's kitchen and bake food that takes hours. He said the two would not have met if it had not been for my class.

"You no come, no come!" Elena told Max, telling him that she was looking forward to spending more time with Kathy and not to come pick her up until morning, and maybe not even then. "I need woman talk with now and then, not man!"

"She get tired of me," explained Max. "I too neat for her. She gets kitchen very messy." So I told him how hard it was for me to work in my own kitchen and how I had given it over first to a cook, and then to Frances.

"Frances look like a very good daughter. And for me--Kathy a *saint*," Max responded. I, who had only seen Kathy as the overweight busybody in my little church classroom, was humbled all over again.

By the time my arm was in a sling I remembered that I had not had any dinner and maybe Max hadn't, either; all I wanted was soup, so we stopped at the Chinese restaurant for takeout and I

226

ordered some egg drop soup. Max chose a couple of other items. He wanted to pay for the food, but I insisted he was my guest.

He also had my prescription filled for me at the pharmacy.

"Sir, this is rather a powerful prescription. You should only let your wife take half a pill until she can be sure of what she can tolerate," warned the woman behind the counter. "She's not that big. How much do you weigh, Madam?" I felt so safe with Max and so amused that she had thought of him as my husband, that I told them my real weight right out loud.

"Huh," said Max. "No wonder I pick you up so easy."

"Mrs. Porter!" A man's voice in the next aisle called to me. "Hey, Mrs. Porter! It's me! Wait up!"

I turned to see who might have overheard me confess my weight, and hurrying toward me was—oh, of all people! My former movie popcorn slinger, Tim. His face was aglow. He stopped short when he saw the sling.

"Mrs. Porter! I am so glad to see you! Oh! Sorry about your—"

"Old war wound."

"Boy, you always were so *funny*! Boy, am I glad to see you! I owe you a vote of thanks." He looked up at Max. "You see, Mr. Porter—"

"This is Max. He's not my husband. Max, this is Tim."

"Oh. Okay! Decided to get out and get living again? All right! How do you do, sir? Well, anyway, Mrs. Porter—I enjoyed our conversations so much at the movies, you know? Boy, you really opened my eyes. You asked me, was I gonna take tickets for the rest of my life? That's what you said. Or did I want people buying tickets to come and see what *I* was doing?"

I said that to him? I just remembered talking about films.

"You were so positive and you just treated me like you had so much faith in me—you were giving me the same lectures that my Mom was giving me, but you were saying them in a different way, so-- so you decided me to go back to school. *Film* school. *You* did it, Mrs. Porter—you kind of primed my pump." Tim stood before me, looking like a freckle-faced puppy wanting a pat on the head. I realized it was the first time I had seen his legs and feet. He'd always been behind the counter.

He reached out as if to give me a hug, then grabbed my left hand and shook it hard instead, carefully avoiding my sling. "Well-- gotta go! Uh—take care of that—war wound thing."

He left the store. Max snorted. "Film school. In this country, they got school for *everything*."

(you must hurry   hurry before I forget my past   before I forget my   unbounded savage dances in the air   my wild beforeness   before they tame me into hopelessness)

228

So now Max and I are sitting on my patio. He has reheated the soup for me in the kitchen and has attempted chopsticks with no success. He has found silverware and bowls for us. The tea he has reheated is jasmine-scented.

I am surprised at how fast he has found his way around my kitchen. "I come here to this country, I work in kitchens. I do anything I can to earn money, bring Elena here."

He looks around. "This is palace. Much family here?" He looks at my face. "No need you tell me about husband. I know story already." He stops. "Man was fool to do what he did." Oh. I wonder if he is thinking of all the refugees taking boats, drowning, to escape the homes of their births, being forced out by the greedy, the lawless, the power grabbers.

"Uh. Just my daughter and my grandson." I hesitate. "They may be moving out. Then it will be just me." (*Until Franklin comes back*, I add silently.)

"Nah. This house not you. Does not look like you. Colors. Where are colors? This not you. Not even kitchen is you. Listen. I am also painter. I paint rooms color you like. Your toes. Colors like that."

(*a flash of peregrine's wings   I am still here   I must fly   I will fly*)

229

I can feel myself blush. Well, I should be embarrassed that he has noticed my feet, but he has said it with no hidden meaning to it. The soup has been a comfort and that half pill is sublime. I can't feel any pain unless I move suddenly.

"Too bad right arm." He makes a motion to show writing.

"No. Actually, I'm left-handed."

"Nah! You? Nah! Me, too." And he grips his table knife with his left hand in an upside-down way as though he is holding a pencil and we both laugh, because we both taught ourselves to write in the same way, even in different countries.

"This house—so big. Small place where I come from." He describes it and I smile, because it sounds like the same size as the house I grew up in, back in Jerome. So we exchange our childhood stories about bedrooms and living rooms and kitchens and bathrooms (him with words and gestures and me with much hesitation and caution, since I have never, ever talked about my past to anyone since moving here to Banana Bay and it is like stumbling, like speaking a foreign language, but such a relief!) and we laugh a lot, only I have to be careful, because if I move suddenly, the now-dull pain reminds me of what I have just been through.

"Why you care what people think, where you come from? We all come from some place. You need be proud. You go to school, you

230

write, you get chance at college—this is to be proud of. You get job. Even people with lots money, they still need job. You. You lucky. You got job as teacher."

"Well. I can't really count that as a *job*. It doesn't pay anything."

"What you love doing, *that* is job."

Maybe I do need a job, I think. I have been moving rather aimlessly, so untrue to my West Virginia laboring roots, waiting this year for Franklin to come home, that I seem to have forgotten to examine my own life.

(I have a sudden image of the peregrine scoffing at me for using the word "aimless". There was *nothing* aimless in her nature as she lunged at the leather cords holding her.)

"Even growing wegetables—*that* is job!"

"You're right, Max." Oh, if only I could confide in him my deep-down darkest fear that all year I have had to hide from everyone, that has taken so much of my energy: that I yearn to agree with them, that Franklin is gone—no. No, I can't. I have to stay strong for his sake even though I am the only one believing this.

"Max, I appreciate all that you've done for me tonight. This was so good of you."

"Nah, nah. You do good for us in class. I return favor. Next time--." He waits for my response. I nod my head and smile. "Yah. Next time I bring wegetables."

231

He rubs his nose, then looks squarely at me. "Miss Maya. You mind I say somet'ing?"

Well, actually I do. I've already today fumbled my class, lost a child, heard about my husband's Huckleberry Finn, gotten an earful of critique about my poetry, a kiss on the mouth from a lesbian, and busted my arm. Oh, yeah—thanks to my husband, I am putting up with a most unusual anniversary.

I remember my manners. "Sure. Why not?"

"Thank you. Okay. Listen. You funny lady. I notice. People say somet'ing nice to you about what you do and you duck head like this." He demonstrates. "That kid in drugstore. He say something nice to you from bottom of heart, he thank you, and what you do? You duck head. Nah, nah. Need to *stand up*. Enjoy good words."

The man is nuts. No. I'm sure I don't do that. "Hey. Are there fortune cookies in that bag?"

"You see? You just duck head!" I blush. Oh. Like that! I have to admit he is right. I never noticed that about me before. "Okay. Okay, I get it. Fortune cookies?"

"I think yah." He turns the white paper bag upside down and two wrapped desserts fall onto the counter. "You pick," I say, the good hostess. He holds them out to me in his left palm and I select one. "Okay. But you read yours first."

Max breaks open his cookie and reads, "Every day for you is blessing." He nods. "Now you."

232

I can't open my cookie with one hand except by crushing it, so Max obliges and unfolds the small strip of paper. He holds it before me, making a show of not peeking at it first. I read out loud, "Do not fly from a surprise."

"Maybe this 'blessing' cookie was for you instead. *I* would like to go on airplane." Ah. He has read the disappointment on my face—I had wanted some more pertinent message about Franklin.

Again, the good hostess: "Where would you go on an airplane, Max?" and he, diverted, starts to list off the places he has not been to, the places he would like to re-visit, the—

(you and I   we were born to fly   we are closer now   ever closer to flying   )

I yawn. "You sleepy from pills. Where you want lie down? I clean kitchen."

"Um-m. I think, actually, on the patio."

So now I am lying here on a chaise. There's a hot mug of jasmine tea at my left elbow. Max has put a blanket over my feet, but it's still a warm evening, so I wriggle out of it and contemplate my painted toes. About forty feet away from me on the other side of Franklin's lap pool there is a big huge man in my kitchen and he is singing and his name is Max and we are both left-handed.

The doorbell sounds. There is a pause and then I hear Father George's voice. I would bet he is surprised at the sight of our new doorman! Now I have two men on the patio. Father George is at my side, a hand on my forehead—not sure if he is taking my temperature or if he is about to bless me. He looks around, wants to know what happened—"And where is Fran? Anybody else get hurt? How about Frankie?"—so we tell him, overlapping, all over again. "Boom! She go down. Boom!" from Max several times, as though I had bounced all over the alley.

Father George has swapped his clerical collar tonight for a natty blue print sports shirt and jeans. Dressed this way he looks like a—well, a regular person. He smells of aftershave. "Now tell me again where Fran is, please?"

"Well, they wanted her to stay to finish their game and then she was going to get them something to eat and then meet us at the hospital, just in case I was   spending the night there." Max is nodding.

"Your daughter is a remarkable person," Father George says. "And your grandson, too. Remarkable people. You are so fortunate."

(my life is mine to use   I still remember how to fly   first let go climb up into the air from this quicksanded earth   let go what holds   let go and FLY   )

No, I tell the peregrine. I cannot. She ignores me. She has somehow become taller, stronger, even more imperious since I first saw her in her imprisonment. She is yanking at her leather strapping, biting at the wooden perch, clawing at the ring around her leg, which looks vaguely like a wedding ring—is she then married to Miss Betsy? Or to one of the owls? How could that be? Will her eggshells be strong enough?

"You look a little woozy," Father George peers at my eyes. "Are they huge?" I ask, smiling because he is so close to me, thinking I could reach up, pull him to me and kiss him—and then remembering that I only have one hand. "Are they as big as the peregrine's?"

"I don't know about that," he says. "How are you feeling?" Oh, his eyes are so blue! It's the best part of his features. His brow is furrowed. Could he really be that worried about me? I'm almost ashamed that I wanted to kiss him. Maybe I should kiss Max instead.

I would entertain that idea, except that the peregrine keeps interrupting me. No, I say in my head to the peregrine falcon, which does not cease her thrashing about, trying to loose herself. No, I have not decided. Someone else needs to make this decision for me.

If she continues to pluck this way she could make herself bleed! "Don't hurt yourself!" I cry out loud, startling my guests.

"Reliving the bowling accident," Father George nods to Max, evidently using all of the psychology 101 he knows. God, the man is stuffy! Hard to picture him naked.

Of course then I picture him naked. I laugh out loud. "Did I just laugh out loud?" I ask. One of my male nurses pats my left hand. "You were fortunate you didn't injure yourself worse." Oh, there's Father George for you. The high road. He hasn't yet prayed over me.

"Yes," I say, "Yes. I am fortunate."

"Maya." Oh no. Listen to his tone of voice. Father George is going to say something to me that I do not want to hear, "About Franklin--."

"Who this Franklin?" Max asks.

"Maya's husband." Father George says.

"Okay. I go. You talk."

"Oh, no, Max. It's nothing personal, is it, Father George?" Oh good, I have cornered him. He's not going to say anything of family matters in front of Max.

"Well. It's—Fran has asked me to talk with you concerning Franklin's memorial service--."

Max looks confused, so I explain. "I haven't yet had a memorial service at the church for my husband Franklin, because he's returning any day now."

Max turns to Father George. "Why she say this? Nah. Nah." Back to me: "You need let him rest in peace. No good waiting all this time for nothing, for nobody. You cry, grieve, you let go, you go on—go forward." He points. "Or stay stuck."

He talks to Father George as if I am not present. "Bad thing to wait for somebody come back. *They* get to stay important and the one praising them all the time gets to be nothing more than—flag waver for them."

Oh, how have I let this outspoken man into my house, spouting philosophy? Acting like my unnecessary superego.

Father George nods. "I've been telling her this all year, Max." Now it is my turn to be cornered, and by these two visitors. One more and they could be self-styled Magi.

"Um—may I have some more hot tea, please, Max?"

He understands that he is being dismissed. "Not my place tell you what to do. Nah. I just know about my Mama and Papa. They not want Elena and me to be stuck. If we stay stuck, then—," he gropes for the right words—"then we not *honoring* them. We saying to them, 'Pah. You give us life. You give your lives. We not care.' Their lives for what? So Elena and me to say what they did has no *meaning* to us? Nah. *Got* to have meaning, or—why?

"We had service for them here. Father here got people to come. Good service. Good idea he had. I thank him for that. Now we finished, they rest in peace, we cry. Oh, we cry! Then we go on. Best thing to do." He stops as tears fill his eyes. "Good man." He impulsively hugs Father George, who I know is used to this from his parishioners, just not such an oversized one.

"Miss Maya. You *wrong*. I get you new cup tea." He grabs up my mug in a kind of rough anger and stomps away from the patio. Father George stays thankfully silent. I feel chastened. Also, I'm worn out from the day's happenings and I'm rather giddy from the drugs. I don't want to have to play hostess right now.

"Well, uh, Maya—nice plantings you have here around the pool. It's so pleasant here at night. You can smell the night-blooming jasmine."

"Um. Manuel insisted on that one. Franklin picked out the others. I'm afraid I don't know much about--."

There's a murmur of voices inside the house. Father George smiles and pricks up his ears like a Doberman. Frankie comes bursting onto the patio. "Wow, Maya, you went *down*!" he yells. I throw up my left hand against him so he won't accidentally hit my right arm and the movement makes me wince. "Careful there," I say.

"Frankie. I bet you're taller than when I saw you last week," Father George says to the boy, who has not taken notice of him yet.

Frances hurries onto the patio. I watch her eyes light up as she sees Father George. "George," she moves to him and gives him a hug. He—why, he actually—blushes! "Fran," he answers, leaning down to kiss her on her cheek.

Wait a minute. Are they just being friendly or—Oh lord. Just how long has this been going on? I wonder. Have I been so preoccupied? For an entire year?

"Maya, have you had anything to eat?" Frances tilts her head toward the house. "There's that lifesaver of a Max in my kitchen and he just apologized to me for breaking a cup."

"A cup?"

"He's mad at something. Was he safe to leave alone?"

"He's like a giant!" adds Frankie.

"Which cup?"

"Oh—just a cup. A mug, maybe."

I am relieved. The last thing I need in the kitchen is a large angry man with access to Franklin's mother's china. The idea of Max as an overgrown bull in a china shop makes me sit up fast. I wince from the uncomfortable motion.

"Maya, don't you have any pills to take care of the pain?" Frances asks, alarmed.

"Yes. I can get them. No, no, not you. I can go get them myself."

Actually, I have not been to the bathroom in hours and was too shy in the hospital to ask Max to accompany me as far as the door of the ladies' room. I asked the female technician to help me instead when I had my arm x-rayed. Maybe the prescription I'm taking is making my bladder feel full. Or it could be all the tea.

We move into the house. I make my way carefully up the step and into my bedroom while the others (save for Frankie, who has run into his room after asking and already knowing the answer, if he could go swimming—"Not without me," said his mother, "Time for bed." and that was that) drift into the living room. Even in the bathroom I can hear Father George at our piano, but I can't make out what the song is. He's really good at playing.

One half pill—that's what Max had allowed me. "Until you know," he said. But it hasn't even seemed to touch the pain. I'll try the other half.

As I come out of the bathroom someone knocks on the bedroom door. Max pops his head into my bedroom. "You okay? They ask me to see—oof!" He has noticed the painted walls. "Who did this? This not right color for you! So much gray make you sad. Look like prison. I been in nicer gulags." This man, I have begun to notice, wears his opinions right out there for all to see.

"I agree, Max. But my husband—it needs to stay this shade for him."

(give me the color of the sky, sings the peregrine into my ear
gray would anchor me to the mud   I must needs be closer to
the heavens than to anywhere else)

Funny. She is louder now. Closer. Hypnotizing me with that huge all-knowing stare.

"So why you not decide for yourself?"

Well. Enough is enough. Now this persistent man is commandeering my bedroom. Just because I let him take me to the hospital. "Max--."

"I tell you—I am painter," he protests. "When you want—I do." I wait until he leaves and then I take an entire pill, the pain is so severe.

The body must not have any sense of time, I think. That broken bone in my left hand—it's as though it just happened. This is what must happen to people with PTSD, reliving an event over and over again, because the body has no idea of time.

This is such a riveting idea to me that I think I must share it with the partygoers out there; but as soon as I have thought it, it is gone. "Gone in evanescence," I say out loud, waving my left hand around like the queen. Oh, I am so in love with that word evan—evan—something.

There is so much conversation going on in the living room that I decide to walk out onto the patio. What a strange day so far, all these different people in and out of my house! And for the entire year before, how many of Franklin's friends ever came to visit me, to console me, even to send me a damned *card*? Hah!

I have not had my vodka martini tonight. Even so, I step down ver-y care-ful-ly onto the patio after I open the French doors. These pills might mess with my balance and there's no sense taking chances and hurting my other arm.

Two broken wings. How would I fly?

 I sit on the chaise where I was sitting before and I adjust my blue hospital-donated polyester sling, again gasping from the movement. How will I manage to sleep tonight? I might have to sleep sitting up.

"The peregrine with its high speed stooping" (that means 'diving', but I love the image of a 'stoop') *"is like a bobsled team tucked tightly together."* I read that recently. It was good that I met that falcon. It got me to the library to read about it, and this had nothing to do with Frankie's report. I had become interested in the bird myself, the first time in a year truly captured by another's life outside my own.

"Tucked/Tightly/Together"—what a poem that would make! That's how the peregrine can make such a sharp angle of attack without harming itself.

The peregrine, I read swoops down on its target from a height. As it descends it extends its feet until they are right under the bird's breast. It clenches its toes, with the long hind toe reaching below the three other toes, which are bent up and out of the way. Moving downward at a great speed, the falcon passes almost near enough to the target bird to touch it, gashing it like a sharp dagger with the hind toe and killing its prey immediately. At the same moment of impact the falcon raises its wings above its back. It is actually a merciful killing. To be hit from a great height so fast by a peregrine weighing between one and one-half and two and one-half pounds would knock the prey senseless.

And "peregrine"—the word means "wanderer". All over the world, no home. Oh, of course they have homes. They make homes for themselves. Poor Franklin, wandering home in his boat from South Carolina. And then wandering in his amnesia.

This is the thing about fantasies so like the ones in movies: they don't hold up well under the probing of reality, like: who has been caring for him? (I picture a sweet-faced nurse, a Meryl Streep, bending over him in his hospital bed to tend him, asking him to try to remember, just try—he must have a family somewhere.

Does he remember anyone's name yet? And he, gazing up at her, struggling to pronounce, "Mayetta Jane, Mayetta Jane"--.)

No. He never called me that. I have always been Maya to him.

(naught else matters   the glory of the sky awaits my shining claws, the arc of my wings)

These are really smooth pills. I can hardly hear the piano. Are they *singing* in there now? Nobody has ever sung at our piano. And yet I can hear Max's voice. What an unusual man.

Another voice. Father George. And a third—Frances. How long since she's sung, except on Sundays in church. And me—where has my voice been all year? Oh, they are like sirens on the rocks, calling Franklin home, past the shoals, like a lighthouse—oh! What wonderful marvelous people, to call him home to me!

I must admit I'm having a hard time remembering right now what he looks like. When I close my eyes all I can see is that bound-up bird.

(I sing because I must   I must fly, even once   I MUST   )

The water in the pool is so yummy enticing dark. That's because no one has turned the light on in it. That's actually kind of neat, not to be able to see what's in it or see the bottom. If you can't see it, then it doesn't exist. Oh, that's funny! I need to tell that to my class. . . What was it I was going to tell them?

(MY life to decide   I am so powerful and strong up here, the wind bowing to my command   one more glorious stoop   )

Maybe I could just see what my Ocean Water toes look like underwater. What did Franklin's toes look like? Did fishies nibble at them? No fishies here.

(one time   one opportunity   one chance   one free dive, unfettered   just once   just once   JUST ONCE   )

Ooh. This water is actually quite warm. I could—ooh, look how my dress billows when it fills with water. Isn't that beautiful! I am my own parachute. Who was Hamlet's girlfriend? I've never understood how she could just walk herself into the river and drown. It seems like literary license to me. Utterly romantic: only because a *man* wrote it. What self-respecting woman, even crazy over Hamlet, that self-absorbed prick, would get her hair tangled in *branches*?

I could edge just a lit-tle ways more. No wonder Franklin loves swimming. Oh! The water holds my broken arm away from my body. It's floating! My sling is like a sail! What a heavenly feeling, to have it so weightless. Yum-m.

This water feels like silk on my body. I need to take this clingy dress off—oof—I can't do it with only one arm. I can only ask Frances. The image of Father George removing my dress makes me redden with embarrassment. Or maybe it's the pills.

The image of Max carefully removing my dress and stepping back to admire my body before he wraps me in his large comfortable-looking arms--I flush in remembrance of when Red and I were—no, I meant to say Franklin. How long has it been since a man has enveloped me in that way? Funny how I want to be wrapped up in a person's loving embrace and the peregrine wants to be free of it?

(NO PERSON must prevent me from flying, from stooping
NO HUMAN

    has that right!   I was born for this)

Franklin, is this what the ocean felt like for you, a year ago? Was the water this warm? Did you think of me, after you sealed your tape recorder, did you have second thoughts that you wanted to tell me about how much you loved me? Did you know that I would work so hard to keep your love alive?

(climbing toward the sun   almost, but not yet   not yet
NOT YET   )

Ah. The water is so friendly, so welcoming. . . I close my eyes. I sink into sleep. I blot out that lofty, condescending, demanding peregrine's voice. .

"WHAT-- WHAT THE HELL ARE YOU DOING?" I yell, gasping, choking up water. I look around at Frances, whose eyes are saucers, at Father George and Max, who are both soaking wet.

"She okay," Max says.

"I choke and gasp. "That's *awful* tea! Too much chlorine in it!"

"Maya, what in the world were you *thinking*?" Frances seems worked up about something.

"I—I forget. Who the hell grabbed my bad arm?"

"Maya, you were underwater!" Frances is patting towels all over me. She is removing my wet clothes with difficulty because I am fighting her.

My teeth are chattering. I am offended. I cough. I am having a hard time catching my breath. What did they do to me? "I was swimming. Franklin was teaching me how to swim."

"Damn it, Maya, you were not swimming! You were *drowning*!" I stare at three humorless faces. I can't believe this—my priest just swore at me.

Well, I've heard that if three people tell you you're drunk, you'd better go lie down. "Is Franklin here? Because I was just talking to him--." Frances snorts. "Okay, I wasn't actually *talking* to him. But I was sure I heard his voice." Although did I actually? Was it Franklin? Was it the peregrine? "Maybe I was talking to myself," I reassure them.

"How many pills did you take?" Father George asks. "Could we have more towels here? Max is really soaked. Max, congratulations. You must have hearing like a dog!"

"Maya. Pay attention. Mother!"

"Frances. Why are you all getting so fussed? Give me back my dress!"

"Oh my god, Maya, do you have any idea what you were--were you trying to join Dad? Commit *suicide*?"

"Anniversaries sometimes do that," states Father George with such certainty that I am all of a sudden quite weary of him. I point at him with a wet finger, "You! Go home!"

The three (ah, *now* I have the Magi. Maya's Magi) burst out laughing.

"He's not going home, Maya. He just saved you, you idiot! He's marrying me and we're going to go home together."

"Actually, we're going to make a home together. With Frankie. And a dog."

"When you get that drug out of your system we'll talk."

"You sure had some dream! Thought you could *swim*!" Oh. Max is still here. And he's wet.

I smile. I hope he admires my figure. *That's* the problem—I should have undressed first. "I *was* swimming!" Really. People have just got to stop laughing at me.

(fly now   wake   awaken   hurry   we must fly now)

Seventeen.

Maya   10:45 pm   May 17, 2019

The Simplest Way   a poem by Maya Porter   2016

The simplest way for us all to stay

In smiling harmony

While we wait our turn in endless lines

At the grocer's, at the bank,

At church communion,

Is to sing. Yes, we could sing. A singalong song,

Not one a professional does. No,

A singalong song, an "E-I-E-I-O" sort of song,

In line at the store, at the bank,

As we pay our last respects. What better way

To show that we all are in harmony,

In family. We simply need to. Sing.

There is a sudden commotion in the living room.

A voice: "Hello? Anybody home?"

Father George grabs Frances' arm. "Are you expecting anyone?" Frances, alert, shakes her head no.

Max: "I go look." He holds out a hand to stop us. He looks grim and protective.

Me, thinking, exultant: *I know that voice!*

Or am I dreaming this whole thing? I didn't dream trying to swim (and I must have failed at it, I guess, because I am so wet.)

Dripping and cautious (I guess they are afraid to leave me alone), we four move to the living room. Max, Father George and I are wrapped in towels. Frances, motherhood written all over her, seems ready at any moment to rush to Frankie's room and protect him. Max looks ready for a fight.

A man, a stranger with red hair almost the color of Frances' and Frankie's, with an unkempt beard, badly wrinkled clothing and dirty shoes, has sprawled himself heavily across the virginally white linen Sofa. We can't see his face, just part of his profile; and the beard covers most of that.

An old man with a shock of snowy white hair and a take-charge demeanor moves as determinedly toward us as his cane will allow. A third man, tall, black, bald—*Punjab!-- Little Orphan Annie!*--the Sunday comics come back to my remembrance— nope, no turban—wearing dark sunglasses, has helped the older man wordlessly down into the sunken living room and then has retreated to stand in front of the draped windows as he scans the room. No emotion shows on his countenance.

Sunglasses again. Like Peggy. Maybe there's a black eye under there.

I am so pleased that I recall the word "countenance"! I am about to laugh out loud when there is the sound of a "r-r-rp!" as the bearded man's belt buckle drags across the fabric of the Sofa, tearing it, *scaring it!*, I note in amazement. Whatever he has used to dye his hair has rubbed itself onto the pillows of the sofa, which appears to be finally, genuinely beaten. Cowed.

"Not so brave any more, are you?" I boast to the sofa. Wow! It doesn't intimidate me anymore! "You dumb old sofa!" I grin like a four-year-old. The man who has just tamed it laughs as though it's all a big joke to him.

(I assume, looking back, that this exchange takes place in just a few seconds, but for me time has become rubbery and stretches itself into slo-ow.)

Well, even so, I can't return the stupid sofa now, I realize, as the white-haired gentleman takes my right hand in his, causing me just a small bit of pain. He stares at me with friendly recognition as he says, "I am so honored to meet you at last, Mayetta Jane McDowell Porter." He pronounces it "Paw-tah".

"We apologize for entering your home at this late hour. We had a tardy beginning to our day and then this one was insistent that we stop at this one particular extravagant restaurant in Orlando."

The man on the sofa groans.

"The only extravagant thing about it, it turns out, was the price. And then he would go no further without imbibing a drink or two to bolster himself, so we were obliged to stop at a roadside bar catering to people on motorcycles, in a place called St. Cloud. Dexter and I of course refused to enter. We waited in the limousine."

"Tell 'em about the band," offers the man on the sofa. Frances, frowning, stares at him. I'm not scared. I feel safe with Max here.

"I prefer not. Loud, raucous music. I'm surprised you could not hear it all the way into Banana Bay. Some untalented group called 'Gail and the Gorillas'--."

Father George and Frances exchange a look. So Father George's ex-wife is still kicking up her heels, just sixty miles away from St. Swithins'.

"And to make a long story short, this unfortunate child had a few thoughtless words with one of the Gorillas and Dexter here, my Man, was called in to settle the disagreement."

We all look at Dexter. He gives no sign that he has acknowledged his name. His eyes in their sunglasses are as hooded as those of the bird at the sanctuary.

"But how do you know my name?" I ask. Really, what an odd day. Has this unusual set of people come to ask us to join them at the vigil on the beach?

A light has started to shine in Frances' face. Father George seems amused now, rather than on guard. The man on the sofa has by now worked himself into an upright position. I get a good look at his eyes, which look ready for fun. He grabs me into a bourbon-soaked embrace while I try to pull away. Someone yells, "Don't hurt her arm!"

"Maya, Maya," the man croons. "It's really me, your --."

I search the faces for Frances. "The pills are doing this, right?" I ask her. But she is crying and laughing at the same time and she has actually yanked the man from me, heedless of my arm, and she is hugging him as hard as she can, sobbing, "Dad! Dad!"

while Father George and Max move back against the glass dining table.

Now the man she calls Dad has broken from Frances' grip to introduce her to the old gentleman as—someone called Franklin Senior. So if I am right, and I will my foggy mind to attend, this is the man who decided to cut Franklin off when he heard we were getting married! Well, I have a thing or two to say to him, if I can only remember what I was thinking. Huh. There is a man who Frances calls Dad here in the room who has just squeezed me and no one will tell me if this is a dream or the pills.

Somebody gasps, a noisy intake of breath. Was that me? No. The gasp is from that elderly man over there, who has taken Frances' face in his hands and is saying "How like your grandmother you look, my dear. Almost a spitting image of her early photos. I must show them to you. Franklin. You didn't tell me." He seems to twinkle. No—he is *glittering*.

"My son insisted that we return before this day was ended, in order to celebrate the anniversary of his disappearance. And there you have it. My apologies. Dexter, will you please get me a glass of water?" Dexter moves to obey as his aged employer sits. *How does Dexter know where the kitchen is?* I wonder. Max, acting as our newest host, disappears into the kitchen to assist.

Franklin. That guy with the beard who has just pummeled the sofa into obedience, is Franklin. So I was right. Here he is. And I, the one who has stood sentinel for an entire year, who has kept a vigil when all else had decided he was gone, who has refused to let down my guard, who has kept the faith when all others had lost theirs—me, Maya Porter, Franklin's muse—I stand dripping onto Franklin's imported carpet, wearing Franklin's towels without the dress he loved seeing me in, now ruined and drenched, me with my beautifully polished toes—once more, thirty-eight years later! In absolute certain triumph I raise my left arm and proclaim in so loud a voice that everyone hushes, even the man in the sunglasses beside the front windows, who hasn't said a word: *"YOU ALL SEE? I WAS RIGHT!"* just before I pass out, fortunately onto my left side, onto the diminished, defeated, deflated sofa.

Eighteen.

Maya   Friday Night into Saturday morning, May 17-18, 2019

I think that I will never stay

In as lovely a town as Jerome, West V.A.

Indeed, if I should choose to ever roam

I'll find no other place to call my home.

(Unfinished and untitled poem by Mayetta McDowell, age 11)

*   *   *

I don't know if anyone gets just how difficult it is to make love when one of the couple has a broken arm; but I did my best. Oh, I was so overjoyed at having Franklin back! But no thanks to the pills, I must have slept through most of the lovemaking.

Franklin's father and the silent (could he be a mute? I mean no offense—I knew a kid in my class back in Jerome who--) Dexter retreated to the Banana Bay Resort Hotel on south Banana Bay Beach. Franklin Senior refused to let us be put out, as he said it.

"We will return in the morning. I will arrange for us to have brunch here at your home and we will take the time to become acquainted even more," he assured us. "I have yet to meet Master Franklin the Second—no, no, don't waken him. I have already had far too much excitement this past hour." His eyes sparkling, he couldn't stop gazing at Frances, the way Franklin had seemed so fascinated by her.

"You imbecile," was all he said to Franklin. "How could you have ever doubted she is yours?"

I wrote down directions to The Katz' Meow, so that they (Franklin Senior!—in my house!—my own father-in-law!) could pick up the food. "It's delicious," I told the two men as they left. Father George insisted on double-checking my map. Then he wrote out another one.

Food: I had been right about bowling alley food. Frankie had complained during the evening of an upset stomach and Frances was letting him sleep as late as he wanted. She herself looked invigorated, even from lack of sleep. She and Franklin had talked for a few minutes or so, introducing Max and Father George to the new group, while I made small talk with Franklin's father, whom I found easy to talk with. I worried that poor Dexter was being left out of the conversation. I figured that maybe he was some unfortunate adopted relative until Franklin in bed later set me straight about the poor man's lack of a tongue. No wonder he couldn't talk!

I guess I had forgotten what a take-charge man my husband is. He brought a kind of high-energy chaos to the house, first singing at the top of his lungs in the shower (I also forgot to go outside to see if his head stuck up as high as the window), and then diving into bed with a huge sigh.

"I'm home," he said to the bed. "Did you miss me?"

I have always loved Franklin's sense of humor, which made me laugh until I had tears in my eyes and my sides hurt. But tonight, I guess because of the pills I had taken, the edge was off my reactions.

"Cat got your tongue?" he asked, patting the bed. "Speaking of that," and that's when he explained to me his conclusions about Dexter.

"Franklin, I broke my arm," I told him for probably the dozenth time.

"So? Just lie there. I'll be careful."

He was careful for the three minutes it took him to finish and then to roll off me and start snoring. I wasn't complaining. He'd told me what a rough two days he and his father had had someplace where they had met up. I thought it was wonderful that Franklin did that for both his father and Dexter, getting them first-class airline tickets to join him in Tallahassee, where Franklin was doing some hush-hush kind of business for the State of Florida. It was just such a relief to know that our government had put him in protective custody all of last year while they hunted down some terrorists who blew up his boat and who would have stolen NASA secrets, if it hadn't been for Franklin; but Franklin hadn't been allowed to contact anyone, not even his family, to let them know where he was. He wasn't even cleared now to tell me where they had hidden him.

I was so proud of him, even though I was miffed that everything had been so secretive. I felt like a fool for having thought that he might have had amnesia—that's the kind of thing for soap operas, not real life, the way Franklin had performed his national duty!

"Franklin," I whispered to him, "you won't believe what a year this has been without you. Don't we have enough money now, so that you can go into some other line of business? Won't the government let you out of whatever contract you signed with them?" He slept on, too deep in sleep to hear me; and I cried a little into the reddish beard of this man who was such a stranger to me.

I dozed fitfully, probably the combination of excitement at having Franklin home, the pills and my injury. Also I hadn't lain beside someone for a year and I had been used to having the bed to myself. I finally slept and this was my vivid dream:

Just as St. Paul in prison found the doors to his cell miraculously open, so do I now stand before the door of the bird sanctuary. The night is black and cool. I am alone here, trembling a little at my audacity, yet determined.

I try the door, which opens easily in my hand, as I knew it would. Inside I have no need of light. I know where I am heading. An owl hoots quietly, once. Twice. There is no other sound save for a bird in a far corner dreamily cooing to itself.

I find her cage and open it. The hooded bird sits, awake, alert, aroused, in anticipation. It is as if we are attached by a tether one to the other.

We are outside in an immense open field. The peregrine perches on my arm, her claws digging into my flesh, but the pain is only slight, is welcome in fact, and I tolerate it, rather surprised—I thought those nails would hurt more than this. Now I remove her hood, trusting that she will wait for my demands, as I will for hers. We stare unblinking at each other, her head free, my mind clear. I know what I have to do. I know what I choose to do.

Remove this, she orders. Remove it--the band around my leg. Hurry. Hurry. Hurry. Smell the air! I work at the band, frowning. She bites at it and at my fumbling fingers.

Listen, I tell her. I must warn you. With your ragged wounded wings—if you stoop from a height just once, you may die.

She fixes me with an imperious stare. I am aware, she says. Now you be aware: this is my life, not yours. It is mine to order. You are earthbound and cannot understand—I was born to fly.

I push apart her white breast feathers with my other hand and feel her beating heart, strong and prepared. She lays her powerful head on my heart in return, just for an instant as I gasp, her gratitude so unexpected.

The band disintegrates in my hand. She rubs at her leg to make sure. That small part of her leg is worn naked, she has borne it for so long. We exchange one last parting look of understanding each other for our wildness, our urgent, ferocious need for freedom. She shudders in preparation on my arm, weighing far less than I thought she would for her size.

And—gone! A keening cry of salutation, of farewell to me, of greeting to the heavens, and she is off, stretching her long-unused wings, beating them, pounding them, testing them against the cool night air.

She tumbles once or twice in the sky as she regains her sense of selfhood so long unused, so long dormant, unchallenged.

She circles me, I think. The night sky is black enough that it is hard to see her anymore; yet suddenly the night is full of stars and then light and the sky has turned from dark gray to the color of clear ocean water and there she is! As high in the atmosphere as I can strain my eyes to follow her!

She is swooping, soaring, making small mock-stoops like a youngster, as if laughing while she re-learns her wings; and although those wings have been injured, they respond to her, reminding her how free she once was, how wild, how utterly, blessedly, unrelentingly wild. Already the memory of the cage's confines are gone. All that matters is now

Now

NOW

Nineteen.

Maya   the next morning   May 18, 2019

The Gravity Tango   a poem by Maya Porter   2017

(to be sung to the tune of "Jealousy" with appropriate hand clapping)

Gr-r-a-vity! (clap CLAP) How dare you make a fool of me! (clap CLAP)

Once I was a-ble to look like Betty Gra-ble.

But now my shape has shift-ed south (clap CLAP)

With every bite that hits my mouth, (clap CLAP)

How is it for the best that my waist meets my chest? (clap clap clap CLAP)

I used to dance all night long to the break, the break of day.

Now in the dark the only place I make my way

Is to the john. (clap clap clap CLAP)

This can't go on! (clap clap clap CLAP)

 I stumble! I grumble! (huge sigh, spoken)— Oy!

I fear that the throw rug will bend

And scatter me on my rear end.

To face so distinkly that I've become wrinkly—

Oh no, not my fault!

It's gravity. (clap clap clap CLAP.)

*   *   *

I want to bring him breakfast in bed. You can imagine how hard that is to do, since I only have the one arm. Frances emerges from her bathroom as I am trying to cut a bagel with one hand. I am wearing the black nightgown I had saved for Franklin. He had, with my insisting, and then my protesting and grimacing as my right arm got in the way, managed to slip it onto me before we made love.

"What are you doing?" she whispers. "Stop before you cut yourself. You look cold. Here, take my bathrobe."

"Thanks. Ooh, nice and warm. How is Frankie?"

"Finally sleeping. He doesn't even know that his grandpa is back. And his great-grandfather! It's like Christmas! Oh, he will be so surprised!"

"You're happy, Frances?"

"Can you tell?" Even though she was up part of the night with Frankie, there's a glow to her. "Imagine, Maya, in the same night Dad comes back, we meet his father and we get to tell all of you together that George and I are going to be married!"

"You know what let's do?" I whisper back, so happy for her. Father George is a little dull, but what the hell—I'm not the one marrying him! "Hey. What do I call him after you're married— George or Father George?"

"Call him 'son'." She and I giggle quietly in a way we have not done in a year. "I'm feeling so light-hearted from last night, but what's your excuse? You still on your funny medicine?" she asks me. "Oh!" she stops. I guess she's just figured out what a man and a woman do when they haven't seen each other in over a year.

I just smile. No use telling her what a -- well, me and my broken arm and my pills—which Franklin seemed overly interested in— he and I will have plenty of time to make up for last night.

"You never lost hope, Maya, did you? I'm so sorry I doubted you."

"A wife knows, Frances. A wife knows."

266

It's at this point, with both of us being so light-hearted, that I take a deep breath and tell her Franklin's secret about working for the government. I don't notice the change in her face as I look around. "Hey, you know what I started to say? Let's celebrate— let's put your Dad's breakfast on his mother's fancy china."

Frances is silent. Being ever so careful, we fix a tray for Franklin. Of course I can't carry it and Frances is ready to do so. She picks it up more roughly than I would have—"Watch it, watch it! We don't dare break those!" and I open the door to the bedroom, which now at last contains my husband. We enter.

Franklin is sprawled in the bed, eyes closed, mouth open. The hair color and the beard give him more the appearance of a satyr, but I know he's mine.

"Franklin?" I say softly.

He jerks awake. He blinks and scowls, stares around the room without seeming to recognize it. I have a moment of alarm—did those government people do something to his brain? Has he had to be this defensive all year in his secret job? Then he spots Frances and smiles. "Thought I smelled coffee," he says. He sits up and pats the bed for his tray and his daughter—the same place he patted for me the night before, I can't help but be amused at noting.

"Sorry. Just glad to be back. It's going to be so nice to drink something that I'm sure nobody's put any additives in."

"Poor Dad," Frances says, an edge to her voice that only I am aware of. "Listen, I hate to run on your first morning at home, but I promised George I'd arrange the flowers for tomorrow's service, and I'd like to finish the job so that you and I can have more time together. I promise I'll be back before your father and Dexter get here."

"Really? They're still in town?"

"Your father knows that it's Saturday, but he said something about checking in with the police chief. And maybe a lawyer. Except he has one he prefers, in Boston."

"He said that, did he?"

"I guess he wants to be sure you don't get another undercover assignment."

He shoots me a dark look. "Maya just told me while we were making your breakfast." She frowns down at him. "It's all safe with me. Frankly, I don't know why I wasn't let in on this a long time ago. All the crying and missing you I did this past year--!"

"Frances, he just didn't want to worry you and he made me promise."

"Even so." She turns away from me to her father. I can tell she's really hurt that I didn't confide in her. I'm bothered that I had had to choose between him and her. How many times had Franklin put me in that position in our lives? "Dad, those times when you were in Europe, away from us for long periods of time—was that--?"

"Yeah. Uh-uh. Wish I could talk about it, but you know--," Franklin tells her. He fixes her with such a raw look of love that I say, "Frances—tell him about your DNA results."

Franklin stops drinking his coffee. "Oh, yes?" he says carefully.

"Yes! Ta-dah! I'm Scottish and English!"

"Huh."

"Well, aren't you happy? Oh, and a little northern African."

"Huh."

"Well, what did you think I'd be?"

"I'm-- well, speechless. I thought with your hair color, you'd be-- .""

"Irish? Maya thought so, too, but no!"

"Mah-yah did?" he drags my name out. "Isn't this something?" I'm appalled. I'm clear-headed enough this morning to see that he's also had doubts all these years!

"Got to run. Oh, Dad, I'm so—I'm so--!" tears well up in our daughter's eyes. I can see she's forgiven him. "Maya never gave up hope!"

"Ya gotta have hope!" Franklin sings at her, parodying the "Damn Yankees" lyrics.

"Listen, Maya, don't give Frankie anything heavy to eat, when he wakes up. Wait until you see him, Dad! You won't even recognize him, he's gotten so big in a year!"

She gives her father one more hug, nearly toppling the tray, and dashes out.

Franklin and I exchange a look. "So-o," he says. "All's well that ends well, eh?"

"Yes indeed," I say. After the tornado that Franklin brought into the house last night, I welcome some calm moments alone with him.

"That was a new sofa I was sitting on out there?" he motions with a piece of toast.

"Uh, yes. See, the old one was--."

"It's a piece of crap. You need to take it back."

I am stunned. "But—but Franklin, you tore it with your belt buckle. I can't take it back now."

I see the subject is over for him. He tears the crusts off the toast, tosses them onto his plate, and shoves the last bit of the toast's center into his mouth. "I'm going to take a shower, then I'm going to check out my car, then I'm going to go in and wake up my grandson," he states. "Maya, you look so different. I don't know what it is." He scans my body, my arm in its sling. "There's a look I've never seen on your face before. Kind of--."

"Relieved?" Oh, and I am as I stand there, drinking him in.

"I was going to say 'wild'—kind of 'out of control'. Not sure it suits you."

Well, I can't take the tray into the kitchen and I can't make the bed with one hand; so I end up taking another half pill for my pain and going out onto the patio to stay out of Franklin's way while he dresses.

"Franklin?" I call into the bathroom on my way out. "If Frankie wakes up before Frances gets back, will you tell me?"

There is no response. I decide I'll lie down in the shade and not go to sleep.

But I have reckoned without the power of the pills. I wake up only because Frances is yanking my good arm. "Maya! Maya, for God's sake wake up!" she is screeching.

"What? What do you want?" I mumble as she actually slaps my left cheek to rouse me.

"It's Dad! Dad!"

"Uh-huh. Your dad is watching Frankie. I just closed my eyes for a minute."

"No! Frankie's still sleeping and Dad is gone! His car's gone! Before Frankie has even seen him!"

I rise up onto my left arm and elbow and squint at her agitated face. "What time is it?" I ask.

"A little after ten. George is here. And that big Max who took you to the hospital is here, too, with some paint samples. He says you told him he could paint your bedroom. Maya, wake *up*!"

"Calm down. Franklin already told me he was going to make sure his car was running. I bet he had a couple of errands to do—be nice if he'd gone to the hairdresser and had that damned beard taken off. Maybe he went to meet his father."

Frances is looking more relaxed. "Sorry. I just—I guess I panicked. I just don't want to lose him again."

"Not gonna happen," I say.

"I mean, once those government people get you on their payroll and in their sights—oh, Maya," she wails, "he looked so *fragile* when he came home last night! What could they have done to him?"

"And it's the government, so we aren't even allowed to ask." I am trying to scratch my head on the right side with my left hand. It's not easy to do. Frances, relieved now, smiles at me. "Have you had breakfast? You shouldn't take those things on an empty stomach."

272

"I ate a couple of toast crusts from your Dad's tray."

"I'll go get the dishes and the tray and I'll fix up your bed for you. Want some clean sheets?"

"Oh, Frances, that would be lovely," I say, a little embarrassed, hoping that Franklin didn't leave behind any traces of our lovemaking. She greets Max, who has just appeared, and she moves into the master bedroom.

"Miss Maya." Max stands on the patio. His demeanor is cautious. "I bring paint colors for you." He adds, "Uh—you not gonna go in pool again? I bring spare clothes for me in car just in case."

"Good morning, Max. Thank you. That's thoughtful. No, no pool for a while. But about painting-- since Franklin has come back, I don't think we need to do anything about that now."

He looks disappointed. "I bring you food that Elena and Kathy make. My sister, she had good time. Also some nice fresh wegetables. Make you healthy." He seems to have drooped some since Franklin's return last night. Well, it's not my job to make everyone happy. "Father George here, too."

Good grief. Are those two men joined at the hip?

Then I hear Frances scream. I make my groggy way into the living room with Max's help. Father George stands in the living room holding onto Frances. She waves some white envelopes in the air. "Not again, not again, not again!" she is crying.

There are four sealed envelopes, evidently from Franklin-- one for me, one for Frances, one for Frankie and the last one for Franklin Senior. The four of us sit down, the men on the ruined sofa, Frances opposite him in her father's leather chair.

Frances opens hers first and reads it slowly and out loud to us. It is a two page letter in her father's inked scrawl and explains at length how Franklin must go away again suddenly, that while I was asleep the government agents came for him with a new assignment. "Frances, love of my life, while they have me on a trumped-up charge I am at their mercy. You will not, unfortunately, be able to contact me, but know that I love you more than life itself and we will never, in our hearts, be parted. There is not a man alive, including the good Father George, who will ever take my place in your heart. Your most loving father, who gave you life and will miss you every moment."

Father George reacts first. "Bullshit."

They watch me as I with difficulty open my letter, which is on a torn-off piece of paper. It contains just five words, although I turn the paper over to see if there's anything else there. I blink. I read out loud, "Maya. You'll be okay. Franklin".

Everyone is watching me. Frances' face looks angry, yet she has tears in her eyes. Mine are dry as I feel a new sensation: something is uncaging my heart.

"Maya. *Mother*. Are you all right?" Frances asks.

"Yes. I will be. Yes."

"Better open Frankie's," Father George recommends. "Spare him any—embarrassment."

Frances rips open the envelope addressed to Frankie and reads to us. In the envelope is the other torn half of my paper and a fifty dollar bill. The message: "Hey there, Frankie. Buy yourself a dog. Love, Grandpa Franklin".

No one says anything. We sit stunned. Then Frances, grim, stands up and walks into the master bedroom. I jump as we hear the crash of a breakfast trayful of expensive china hitting the floor. She returns with my purse. I look inside. I know I had two fifties yesterday. My money is gone. "He can't get far on fifty," I say.

"Fran. Frankie is *not* getting that letter, "Father George says firmly. "That's a damned nasty thing to do to that innocent boy."

Max interjects, "Yah. Who does that to little kid? And what this about government?"

So we explain the witness protection program and Max scoffs. "You Americans with your love of Double-Oh-Seven. Maya, your husband made up story and left."

Frances and I protest, but not too vigorously. "How he leave?" Max persists.

"Uh—he took his car. I think."

"I checked. It was gone," Frances says. There is a new steely edge to her voice.

"Sure it was gone. Government gonna let you keep your own car. Pah," Max says in a voice of scorn. We sit and face the idea that—well, in a word, that Franklin may have lied to us.

The doorbell rings. No one speaks. When Frances answers it she returns with Franklin Senior, Dexter and a cardboard carton of breakfast foods, complete with a single flower in a tiny vase. The elder Franklin seems not surprised at our stories. He takes the letter addressed to him and, without opening it, tears it in two. He looks at Frances and me.

"Have either of you," he asks, "ever left a child out in the rain? Ever dangled one off a bridge?" We are horrified and shake our heads no. "Then you pass the test for good motherhood. Now— when do I get to meet my great-grandson?"

Frances gulps. "I'm afraid, sir—." Franklin Senior regards Frances warmly, "I'm afraid that in my distress I threw some of your wife's expensive china into the trash." She motions to the breakfront. "I'm so sorry. I know it's priceless and I don't know what came over me. I'm really not an irrational--."

"Dexter," the old man says quietly. Dexter, alerted, strides to the breakfront and before even Max can stop him, shoves the immense piece of furniture with one seemingly effortless motion from the wall, so that the dining table and chairs skitter out of its way on the hard glazed white tile. The glass tabletop breaks into two pieces just as though someone had come at it with an enormous karate chop, allowing the breakfront to fall free and shattering the entire collection of china. There is no sound save that of a few hung-up errant pieces of china falling and crashing with a tinkle like a cartoonish aftershock.

We sit in silent disbelief. "Thank you, Dexter," says Franklin's father quietly. Dexter nods and moves back to his self-appointed place beside the front window. Someone has opened the draperies this morning, I notice. The day outside looks bright and shiny.

The phone on the table by the front window rings. At the same moment Frankie appears in the hallway at the living room entrance. He looks across at the destruction. "Whoa! Did we just have an *earthquake*? Wait'll I tell Deano!"

"Watch your feet!" says Father George. Max automatically scoops up the youngster away from the debris. "You so heavy I can hardly lift!" he jokes.

No one is answering the phone, so I make my way to it. Even if Dexter, who is closest, picked it up, what could he say? Frances, still in a kind of shock over the dish debacle, is busy introducing Frankie to his great-grandfather and they are chatting together about the "earthquake".

"Hello. Porter residence," I say, the way Franklin taught me.

"Maya," a familiar husky voice says.

"Brenda?"

"Hey—just checkin' up on you. Doin' okay after last night?"

"Yes. Yes!" I look at my family. Franklin Porter Senior has moved everyone out of the path of the china and glass storm and onto the patio. Max has picked up the huge carton of food to join them. I can hear my father-in-law assuring Frances that he will arrange after we eat to have a crew come in to clean while we all go to the beach. I realize that I'm hungry. I see Father George (I've acquired a father-in-law and a son-in-law in the matter of a single day!) standing, blessing the meal. No, I'm not just hungry—I'm ravenously hungry.

"Hey, Brenda. Thanks for all your help last night at the bowling alley."

"Sure thing. We need you to be there next week to keep teachin' us."

"You—you like my class?"

"Wouldn't miss it." So it's not just the cookies she comes for!

"I'll let you go. Us West Virginia folks gotta stick together. Bye."

"Wait! Wait. Brenda—uh—how'd you know I'm from West Virginia?"

"You kiddin'? With that accent? Spot you a mile off."

I hang up, smiling at Dexter, who does not smile back. Instead he takes my good arm and I turn to join the others on the patio. The dining room looks as though it has been in a hurricane. On this side of the wreckage the sofa sits, looking forlorn. The noise level has risen outside. I can see Frankie re-creating my fall in the bowling lane last evening. "Bam!" reaches my ears as the phone rings again. The docile Dexter lets me go so I can answer it.

"Hey, Brenda," I say

"Hello. Is this--Maya?"

"Yes, it is. Who is this, please?"

"This is Peggy. Uh—you know, from yesterday at the restaurant--?"

"Oh. Certainly. Of course. Would you mind speaking up?" Franklin Senior has just said something that has made Frankie and Frances go off into bursts of laughter

"I'm not sure who is listening in. See, I wouldn't have phoned you, but—oh, I just hate what you will think of me!"

"Oh. Yes?"

"It's—I have confidential information for you about Franklin."

"Ah." I look down. "Huh. This is funny. You're talking to me and here's your card, the one you gave me yesterday." A paranoid thought occurs to me. Did she mean the card as some kind of coded message when she'd handed it to me? "Call me if you need to talk," she'd said. Was that to mean she knew about Franklin's job? "Peggy. Are you also working for the government?"

"What? No! Listen, I should have said this to you yesterday at the restaurant. I was just so mad at him for giving me a black eye that—brace yourself, please, Maya."

"Okay. I'm braced." Him. So a *man* gave her a black eye.

"Oh lord, how do I say this? Franklin's —he's really still alive."

"Were you at Katz' Meow this morning? Is that how you know?" I am confused.

"Maya! I was at his motel room in Sarasota last week!" I have to hold the phone away from my ear at this.

"You don't have to shout, Peggy. I broke my arm, not my ear."

"Oh my god! Did he break your arm, *too*? This man is *dangerous*!"

Franklin Senior has shown up at my side. He gives me an inquiring look. "This woman is saying she's been with Franklin in Sarasota and I think she's either working for the government also or she's lying," I whisper to him.

"Ah. Yes, well—about Sarasota. I will explain when you are through there." My father-in-law looks sheepish. Peggy is still blasting into my ear, "Stay away from him! Stay away from him!"

"Peggy, I'm going to hang up now--."

"What? No! Don't hang up! He's *here*! Franklin's here at my condo, getting in my way while I'm packing! Don't you get that he's *alive*? He's been alive all this time!" I hear a shriek and Peggy swears at someone. "And Amanda's here, checking out my place so she can make an offer on it, and she's all excited about having found him alive, and she figures there's some kind of reward, maybe from his Boston relatives—you know, "Missing millionaire returns", et cetera et cetera. She's about to call the newspaper, but I wanted to let you know where he is first. Aren't you thrilled, Maya? Aren't you *overjoyed* that he's *alive*? Maya--!"

"Well, wait. How do *you* know he's been alive all this time? Let me think--."

"Maya, I don't *want* him here!" She turns from the phone and yells at someone, then comes back to me. "I can't believe it! He's trying to come on to Amanda! Right in front of me! I am just now putting my life back together and I don't want him screwing it up again!" She screams. "Amanda, don't let him *hit* you!"

Franklin Senior squeezes my good arm in a paternal touch. "May I assume it is about Franklin on the phone?" Frances is staring at me now from across the room. *Don't let Frankie know*, I gesture to her. She nods.

I turn back to my father-in-law. "It's about him, yes. I just found out where he is." I give him Peggy's card. This woman is breathing like fire into my ear for the second time in four years. I note she has written the gate code down. It has remained the same: one two three four. *Really.*

She carries on: "I want him dead! I WANT HIM DEAD!" I wait until she takes a breath before I get my few words in, words I find I have waited all my life to utter:

"Peggy—just don't take it personally, but—no, thanks. No More Poor Me," and I hang up on her. I drop, exhausted from the encounter, into a chair.

I look across the room. I swear the sofa shivers. "You're next," I tell it. It can apologize all it wants to, but I am newly unrepentant.

"Peggy says she wants him dead," I announce to Franklin Senior in a light tone intended to keep the people on the patio from knowing how drained I feel. Franklin Porter Senior leans on his cane and beckons to his voiceless Man, giving him Peggy's card. "Maya, you could use some breakfast. Dexter. You know what to do."

Dexter nods.

It takes me a moment to notice that Dexter has left the house, when I look out the window and see him heading for the limousine in the cul-de-sac. I chase after him. It takes me a valuable moment to open the sticking front door with one hand.

"Dexter! Dexter!"

I have to somehow keep him from harming Franklin, although I realize suddenly, in an uncaged-heart kind of way, that I finally concur with Rhett Butler's parting line to Scarlet O'Hara.

I grab the sleeve of my father-in-law's Man. I can feel his muscled arm through the material. "Hey, Dexter. Stop. Wait, please."

He halts obediently at my frantic tugging. I don't know why I wait for him to smile down at me. I have yet to see that face reflect any emotion. He's suited up like those guys who were chasing Neo in that futuristic movie, so maybe that's how they're all trained to look and act.

"Listen, Dexter. Uh. No. Never mind about Franklin Junior. Don't bother. Let's let the government handle him. They'll know what to do."

He doesn't try to loosen my grip. I look up at him, more curious now than scared, trying to peer behind those concealing dark sunglasses, that impassive chiseled face.

"Dexter, I wonder if I might ask a favor of you? Would you get Max and please carry the sofa to the curb so I can call the trash men to take it away?"

There. I have said it out loud, have made a decision. Resolute. That's how I feel. Resolute and a little—(Franklin was right)—out of control. Rather--wild.

What an odd thing to witness: the Franklin I missed was not the Franklin who returned. And I guess the Maya he left was not the same one he returned to.

That might make a poem! "I loved you when you left/And I was all bereft/ Our marriage, how it cleft/--."

Miss Pendleton was right. I do better when I don't try to make it rhyme.

All at once—the shrill piercing scream of a call overhead. Dexter and I look up. Straight up. I shade my eyes with my left hand, my right one trying automatically to join the other, but held back by the sling. I note that the pain is more manageable today.

Dexter points upward, then looks back at me. I see to my disbelief that he has yanked off his sunglasses and his large deep chocolate brown eyes are sparkling, his mouth open wide in a huge joyful grin of even white teeth.

And a tongue.

"It is a peregrine falcon, Miss!" Dexter shouts.

He speaks! Dexter speaks! Dexter is pronouncing his words in a most beautiful, musical *Jamaican accent!*

"Here, Miss. Here." He points skyward while supporting me, a strong hand behind my left arm and onto the small of my back.

"Now. Yes. Now you lean farther back." (I do.) "Don't you worry yourself now. I will not let you fall. I have you." (He does.

284

I feel secure.) "Now see, see way up there, Miss Porter!" (Yes, yes!) "Did you know, Miss Porter, that these truly wondrous, exquisite birds were once almost *extinct*? I myself have actually looked into the eyes of one of these wild creatures of God—no, no, not even caged—no one should ever cage these extraordinary creatures-- and it stared right back at me, oh so bold, so majestic, so knowing! Is it any wonder the kings of ancient worlds worshipped them? Ah, in the village where I was born, where we were so poor, I would go to school and I swear to you, Miss Porter, when. . .oh. I should call you Maya? Then you must call me Dexter, named after the *most amazing* Jamaican composer Noel Dexter—what an *honor* my parents bestowed upon me, Miss Maya. Have you ever been to Jamaica, Miss Maya?. . Oh, but you *must*! You would love it there. . .No! You also were poor as a child?—then we have much in common, do we not? Allow me to tell you about this singular bird, Miss Maya. When I would come home after school I would whistle. And I am telling you the very honest truth, Miss Maya, that this peregrine would *answer* me! Look up there, look! See, it *dances* up there as if it *owns* the sky and oh, what a showing-off rascal! It knows it! What a fine omen! What a stroke of good fortune! Oh, the stories I could tell you!" (He will).

The end

NOTES ABOUT THIS BOOK

For more information about the peregrine falcon, the reader is directed to what is regarded by some as the "gold standard for all nature writing" about this elusive bird in the book "The Peregrine" by J.A. Baker, a fiftieth anniversary edition, 2017 www.harpercollins.co.uk/green. The book was instantly hailed in 1967 as a masterpiece. It was awarded the distinguished Duff Cooper Prize.

This delightful, frustrating, densely word-saturated book by a man who never learned to drive a car, who bicycled into the area around the rural lands of Essex, England, obsessed with peregrine falcons, continues after a half century to attract readers who both love and are consternated by John Alec Baker's observations. No one who reads it remains indifferent to it: it is littered heavily with the corpses of birds and foul weather. It reads as if Baker yearned to become less human and more a peregrine falcon himself and failed at it—but what a magnificent failure!

Baker suffered from rheumatoid arthritis from the time he was young, dying at the early age of sixty-one in 1987 from cancer brought on by the drugs used to help his crippling bouts. An intensely private man, well-read and known for his letter-writing, he met Doreen Grace Coe when she was sixteen. The story goes that she had missed her bus and he rode her home on the handlebars of his Raleigh.

Her father forbade her to marry before the age of twenty-one. She was married to Baker a month after her twenty-first birthday. They had no children. She packed his lunches for him, for his days outside in solitary observing and journaling. They lived a quiet life. They had no telephone and when Baker won his award he was reluctant to give anyone his address, for fear of losing his privacy.

He journaled around the time of Rachel Carson, who had written "Silent Spring" to a global audience about the dangers of losing our bird populations to the widespread heedless spraying of vegetation with DDT and other poisons. Along with Derek Ratcliffe (1929-2005), another British writer/naturalist fervently passionate about the link between pesticides and the thinning of eggshells, especially in the peregrine population. Baker urged us not to be "soothed by the lullaby language of indifferent politicians". His rage to their indifference can be felt throughout his book.

His book is taught in universities to this day.

The eminent moviemaker Werner Herzog requires his film students to read three books: a Virgil, a Hemingway and "The Peregrine". Herzog refers to the author as "ecstatic", meaning that like a mystic, Baker succeeded in becoming one with the peregrine.

The peregrine falcon I wrote about actually lives in a bird sanctuary in Apopka, just north of Orlando, Florida. The story about mice that overran a new housing development, and its subsequent owl solution, is one I heard there.

I still have dreams of setting the peregrine free for one last grand and glorious stoop, as she was born to do.

Barbara Bayley

October 2019

Here's the A.A. Milne poem that got Mayetta Jane interested in poetry:

<u>The Old Sailor</u>

There was once an old sailor my grandfather knew

Who had so many things which he wanted to do

That, whenever he thought it was time to begin,

He couldn't because of the state he was in.

He was shipwrecked and lived on an island for weeks,

And he wanted a hat and he wanted some breeks;

And he wanted some nets, or a line and some hooks

For the turtles and things which you read of in books.

And, thinking of this, he remembered a thing

Which he wanted (for water) and that was a spring

And he thought that to talk to he'd look for and keep

(If he found it) a goat, or some chickens and sheep.

Then, because of the weather, he wanted a hut.

With a door (to come in by) which opened and shut

(With a jerk, which was useful if snakes were about),

And a very strong lock to keep savages out.

He began on the fish-hooks, and when he'd begun

He decided he couldn't because of the sun.

So he knew what he ought to begin with, and that

Was to find, or to make, a large sun-stopping hat.

He was making the hat with some leaves from a tree,

When he thought, 'I'm as hot as a body can be,

And I've nothing to take for my terrible thirst,

So I'll look for a spring, and I'll look for it first.'

Then he thought as he started, 'Oh, dear and oh, dear!

I'll be lonely tomorrow with nobody here!'

So he made in his note-book a couple of notes:

'I must first find some chickens" and 'No, I mean goats.'

He had just seen a goat (which he knew by the shape)

When he thought, 'But I must have a boat for escape.

But a boat means a sail, which means needles and thread;

So I'd better sit down and make needles instead.'

He began on a needle, but thought as he worked,

That, if this was an island where savages lurked,

Sitting safe in his hut he'd have nothing to fear,

Whereas now they might suddenly breathe in his ear!

So he thought of his hut... and he thought of his boat,

And his hat and his breeks, and his chicken and goat,

And the hooks (for his food) and the spring (for his thirst)...

But he never could think which he ought to do first.

And so in the end he did nothing at all,

But basked on the shingle wrapped up in a shawl,

And I think it was dreadful the way he behaved...

He did nothing but basking until he was saved!"

A.A. Milne, "The Old Sailor" from his book of poems "<u>Now We are Six</u>"   first pub. 1927

E.P. Dutton & Co., Inc., New York

Barbara Bayley lives in Melbourne, FL. She is a church organist and a prize-winning playwright.

This is her seventh book. Her first book, <u>I Could Always be a Waitress</u>, was published under the pseudonym B.J. Radcliffe.

Her other books are:

<u>Your End of the Boat is Sinking</u> (autobiographical)

<u>Something to Draw On</u>

<u>All Creatures of our G.O.D. and King</u>   (with Father George as its main character)

<u>Hoarding: No Place to Sit Down</u>

<u>The Easy Way Out.</u>